LUCIFERIN

I0544647

J. Peter W.

GRINDHOUSE
PRESS

For my daughter who brought home a book about fireflies and sparked the idea of this strange story.

ONE

"STOP PULLING MY LEG," NATALIE says. She's examining my eyes, searching for signs of a bluff. "That can't be true."

"I'm being serious. It's always dark there. Day or night."

"Bullshit. That kind of thing only happens in, like, Canada or Alaska. No way a small town in southwest Virginia gets shit like that."

"It's not like Alaska. It's not seasonal dark. It's like the sun stops existing once you cross into town."

She looks like she's about to say something more when a horn blares from behind us. I look into the rearview mirror and see some obnoxious jackass waving his arms around like he's on fire. I glance up at the stoplight; it's green and I'm first in line. I put my hand out the window and wave as politely as possible to the jackass, letting him know I'm aware of the issue. Then, when the light turns yellow, I slowly proceed through the intersection making sure he has to run red or wait another cycle.

1

"Jackass." Natalie moves her attention toward the road.

"Yeah, I know, right? The nerve of some people."

"I was referring to you." She smiles slyly.

"What? That? Just teaching him a lesson on manners." As the words leave my mouth, a plastic Taco Bell cup filled with what smells like Baja Blast Mountain Dew smacks me across the face and spills all over my lap. I recognize the same horn honk and the obnoxious jackass drives by yelling something incoherent. I nearly turn us into the ditch.

"Watch it!" Natalie reaches for the steering wheel, but I set us straight before she gets to it.

"Fuck." I pull my phone out of my jeans pocket. My entire lap is saturated in shitty soda. I click it on, making sure it still works.

"Guess it's you that just learned a lesson," she says, wiping droplets from her face and shirt.

"Ha-ha, very funny. Fuck that asshole." I set my phone up on the dashboard and rub the sting from my eyes.

We still have a two-hour drive ahead of us and I hadn't planned on stopping the rest of the way, but I can feel the Mountain Dew seeping into my briefs. "I need to pull over and get cleaned up."

Natalie nods but doesn't say anything. I wonder if she's thinking about my hometown. She's the first girlfriend I've ever mentioned the place to, and if it would have been avoidable, I wouldn't have.

I shift in my seat, looking around at the mostly empty fields surrounding us. There isn't a single place in sight. We drive in silence, and I feel like more of an idiot with each passing, pants-soaked minute. Finally I see a sign promising gas and snacks just six miles ahead. *Get to Willie's Weenies and you've gone too far!*

"Shit. Six miles."

Natalie nods again and then reaches for the radio. She fiddles with the tuner until she finds a guy with a thick southern accent talking about ghost hunting. It sounds like three hillbillies wandering around a dark basement.

I see the gas station in the distance. I slow until I reach it, pulling in like I'm casing the place as I look for a bathroom. It's one of those you can enter from the outside so I park on the side of the building. There's a rather large lady standing beside the women's door. She's wearing a stained Nascar shirt and green neon leggings so tight I wonder how she ever got inside of them. Something is weird about her hair, like maybe she found a discarded wig in a nearby dumpster and decided it was salvageable.

"Don't take too long." Natalie pulls out her phone and starts scrolling through Twatter or Facepalm or one of those sites.

"It'll just be a minute."

I cut the engine and grab the plastic cup. I can see the lady watching me as I step out of the car. In the direct sunlight, the Mountain Dew stain is even more obvious. I try to brush it off for some reason, like the dark, soaked spots will fall away if I hit them at the right angle. I check my seat, thinking there will be a large puddle, but it looks like most of it soaked in my jeans. Then I shut the car door and walk toward the building.

"You smell nice," the large lady says.

"Huh?" I see her eyeing my crotch.

"Baja Blast?" she asks, her nostrils flaring.

"I guess." I shrug and walk to the men's room, dropping the plastic cup in a trash bin by the door. The stink of a gas station bathroom in the middle of summer can only be compared to wearing a urine-filled toilet as a hat. I gag but catch myself before any vomit can make its way up my throat. The sink has red markings along the rim. I wonder if it's blood, making sure to avoid any contact. The water comes out in a tiny trickle no matter how far I turn the handle. I cup my hands beneath it and try to scoop out a decent amount, then sort of slosh it onto my pants. It's messy, but gets the job done. I turn off the water and look for paper towels. Of course there aren't any. No blower either. I wonder if I would have been better off letting the soda dry on its own.

When I get back outside the lady in neon pants is standing next to my car.

"Can I help you?" I ask her.

She's eyeing Natalie, who is oblivious to the whole thing. "She's a pretty one."

"Uh, thanks." I slide between her and the car, opening the door as much as I can. "Excuse me."

The large lady takes one step backwards, but that's it. She watches me struggle to get inside, tilting her head slightly as if she's having trouble figuring out what I'm doing.

"What the hell is she looking at?" Natalie asks, finally seeing her.

"I don't know." I get situated, shut the door and turn on the engine. "But she's been watching you for a few minutes."

"Nice." She puts her phone away as I back out of the parking spot.

"They probably don't get a lot of visitors around here." I give the creepy lady a nod as we pull out of the gas station.

"No shit."

We don't get far before my phone rings. I grab it off the dashboard and check to see who's calling. I close my eyes and exhale, then look over to Natalie. "It's my sister."

She turns the ghost hunter show down. "What does she want now? She better not be bailing on you."

"She won't." I lift the phone to my ear. "Hey."

"Hey, are you close yet?"

"I just left an hour ago. It takes three hours to get there, Deborah."

"Okay. You could've just said no. Why are you getting all atti-tudey with me?"

"Did you want something?"

"I want to get the fuck out of this house. Mom is freaking me out and Dad is gone."

"Calm down. What do you mean gone? He's not supposed to leave the house. Is he wandering around the woods?"

"I don't know. He's just fucking gone. I saw him in his reclin-er and then I turned around and he was gone."

"Goddammit. You're supposed to keep an eye on them until I get there. How the fuck do you lose an eighty-year-old man?"

"Don't yell at me, Daniel. I didn't even want to be here. I'm doing the best I can."

"They're your fucking parents, too. The least you can do is watch them for a few hours."

"Well if you would have paid the fucking nurse she would still be here and I wouldn't have to deal with this shit."

I catch my words. I want to yell at her, but I know there's no point. Deborah is as unreliable as they come. I knew that before I asked her to watch them. I knew she couldn't afford the nurse's monthly payment either. I guess I can only get so mad. "We'll be there in two hours. Don't take your eyes off Mom." I click off the phone before she can reply. Fuck. I hate dealing with this shit as much as she does. Goddamn nurse. I'm late with the payment one time and she fucking takes off. I'm gonna file a complaint on her ass.

Natalie turns the volume up on the show, folding her arms across her chest. I can tell she's pissed off. A week ago we were supposed to be going on a vacation to Myrtle Beach. Instead, we're going to take care of my parents in the shittiest, strangest small town in Virginia.

TWO

"TELL ME ABOUT IT," NATALIE says, stretching and shifting in her seat.

"About what?"

"Besides the constant darkness. What else? I don't really have a clue what I'm getting into."

"I don't know. Uh, well, my parents still live in the house I grew up in. It sits about a half mile off the closest road and even farther from any neighbors. The land around the house is mostly wooded, besides a small barren field to the east of the house, where I was told an old church and cemetery used to be. I never saw any of that, but my parents told me repeatedly and reprimanded me whenever I got close, like the field was sacred or something.

"As soon as I graduated high school, I left and haven't returned for more than a day visit. Even back then the town was barely alive. When Lucid Light—a hi-tech imaging corporation—shut down, the whole town started to fall apart. Deborah was pretty pissed when I ditched out. She ended up running away with one of her boyfriends a few months after I left. We only speak when it involves Mom and Dad or her looking for money."

"Sounds nice," she says. Her phone vibrates and she swipes the screen, going through her messages.

I pull off the main highway. I can see the town in the distance to the left, but stay right onto a mostly deserted road. "I told you, always dark." I point to a ragged-looking sign that reads: *Welcome to Luciferin.*

Natalie looks up from her phone. "It's ten o'clock at night. Of course it's dark. I watched the sun set an hour ago."

"You'll see."

Even though there's no sun here, the dark sky is lit up with lights. The stars are always shining, and at night, the fireflies come out.

A half mile in, she rolls down the window and leans out, reaching for the bugs. "I've never seen this many in one place before. It's like the stars came down to visit."

"It still feels like an infestation to me. I remember one summer when there were so many it was hard to walk outside without them landing all over you."

Natalie sits back in her seat, cradling a firefly in her palm. She watches it crawl across her skin, blinking bright yellow.

A few minutes later, I pull up to the driveway, but stop in the middle of the road. I see my dad. He's completely naked and riding on a stick like it's a hobbyhorse. He's skipping down the driveway, slapping his bare ass and shouting giddyup. I consider my options: Keep driving down the road, pretending I can no longer find the place, ignoring the inevitable calls from Deborah, and think of my family as non-existent from that point on. Or the easier, but much messier option: run over Dad with the car.

"What the heck is that man doing?" Natalie starts laughing uncomfortably.

"That man is my dad and it looks like he's pretending to ride a horse, naked."

"That's your dad?"

"Yep."

I pull up slowly, stopping the car once I'm fully in the driveway. I get out and stand next to the door, watching the old man do his thing. Part of me is envious of the freedom he has. His mind is so far gone he actually believes he is riding on a horse. I don't have the slightest idea why he's naked though. I'm sure it has something to do with his cowboy delusion. Whatever he's doing, he has no care in the world, completely oblivious to everything and everyone around him.

"Hi, Dad."

"Giddyup, cowboy!"

"You want a ride back to the house?"

He winks at me and I suddenly wonder if this is all an act. Maybe he hasn't lost it at all. Maybe he just wants us to think that. "I'll take Perdy. She's gorgeous, ain't she?" He pets the side of the stick as if he's rubbing his hand through a golden mane. "Meet ya there! Giddyup!" He turns and slaps his flat, sagging ass once more, skipping up the driveway to the house.

"Right behind you." I get back in the car and follow after him, wondering if he really is going to go home or if he'll suddenly dart off into the woods.

"Seems nice," Natalie says. I can tell she's stifling a laugh.

"Sorry I didn't mention his ..." I search for the words. "Issues before."

"When you said they were ill, I was picturing sickly, bedridden. Not . . . that."

"Yeah, I guess I kinda left that out."

When we get up to the house, I see Deborah standing on the

porch, nervously chewing on black-painted fingernails. She has twice as many tattoos as the last time I saw her and her hair is dyed purple. When we get close, she comes down to meet us.

"How the fuck did he get naked?" Deborah says. "Where are his clothes?" She walks up to Dad, shielding her eyes from his flopping penis and scrotum.

I turn off the ignition and step out of the car. "Are you seriously asking me? I just got here."

"He was wearing them earlier." She grabs his upper arm and leads him to the front door.

"I guess he tossed them in the woods. I don't know, like I said, I just got here."

"Whatever." When she gets him to the porch, she tries to take the stick, but he starts neighing at her like he's vocalizing the horse and she's hurting it. "Let it go!"

I watch them struggle for a few minutes until Deborah finally gives up and goes inside. Dad skips in a circle as if he's trying to calm the horse down. "Whoa! She's gone, Perdy. She's gone." He starts petting the stick again.

"Is this really happening?" Natalie gets out of the car.

I go over to Dad and put my arm on his shoulder. "Come on, Dad. Let's bring Perdy inside."

He nods and starts up the porch steps. I see Natalie slowly making her way to the house. I wonder if she would be driving away right now if I'd left the keys in the car.

Inside, I let Dad go and he makes his way to the lounge chair. I see Mom sitting on the couch mumbling. I go in to hug her and she whispers in my ear. "Slugs are in the flower bed. Slugs are in the flower bed."

"Hi, Mom."

"She's been like that since I got here," Deborah says. "Did you know she'd gotten that bad?"

"That fucking worthless nurse never told me shit. We only

spoke when she wanted her paycheck."

"So that's the chick you been shackin' up with?" Deborah points behind me.

Natalie is standing half in and half out the front door. She looks like she just walked in on an orgy.

"Deborah, Natalie. Natalie, Deborah."

Natalie waves meekly, still looking terrified and uncomfortable.

"Why the hell would you bring her along?" Deborah goes into the kitchen.

I wave Natalie inside, then follow Deborah. "We live together. We do everything together. She's practically family now, so get used to it." I get a glass from the cabinet, filling it with water from the tap. I take a small sip and then spit it out in the sink.

Deborah starts laughing. "Tastes like asshole, doesn't it?"

"What the hell? Is the septic leaking into the well?"

"Fuck if I know. Do I look like a goddamn plumber?"

"That's the last thing we need."

"We?" She picks up her hemp-weaved purse. It's covered in retro band buttons with a weird giraffe skull patch on the side. Then she plucks her keys from the table. "I was only here to watch them until you got here. I can't handle shit like this. Besides, you don't need me, you've got your girlfriend." She opens the back door and starts down the steps. Her green VW Beetle is parked behind the house next to the old oak with the tire swing we used to play on as kids.

"Wait!" I chase her to the door. "You're bailing on me?"

"You'll be fine." She hops in the car and starts it, peeling out in the grass as she speeds away before I can protest anymore.

"Bitch." I hope she dies in a fiery accident.

I go back inside. Dad moved from the chair to the couch, he's still holding the stick and petting it. He's wearing a bathrobe. I don't know if he got it himself or if Natalie put it on him. The television is on but muted. I don't realize its porn until I'm sitting on the couch between him and Mom. They are both staring forward, watching the screen.

Natalie is still standing, though she is fully inside now and the door is shut. I don't think she can see the television from where she is. I give her a quick smile and look back to the screen.

A middle-aged, pot-bellied man is choking a young girl as he thrusts into her. I look around for the remote and find it on top of the television. Just before I stand up to get it, Mom starts laughing. It's not her usual laugh; this is more theatrical. Then Dad joins in, throwing his head back and pointing at the screen. "Johnny, you dog!"

Mom pulls a white handkerchief out from between the cushions and starts dabbing it under her eyes. She's laughing so hard now I think she might keel over and die.

I stand up and go to get the remote, quickly turning it off before Natalie realizes what's on. The second the screen goes black, Mom and Dad stop laughing. It's almost instant. I look back at them, standing in front of the television. Their eyes are in my direction, but not focused on me. They seem sad. I decide to turn it back on, setting the remote back on top of the television. Right away they start laughing again.

Natalie takes a few steps forward so she can see what they're watching. "Jesus." She turns away, covering her mouth.

"I need a beer." I cross the living room and head into the kitchen. I pull open the refrigerator, but it's empty of anything besides milk and eggs, and a handful of questionably old condiments. I pace the kitchen twice and then go to the backdoor. "I'll be back in a minute, don't go anywhere."

"What?" I hear Natalie shout, but I'm already outside and don't stop. "Daniel! Where are you going?"

THREE

THERE'S A CONVENIENCE STORE JUST a couple of miles from the house. I've only been in it a few times, despite growing up so close. I'm happy to see it's still there and open. It looks like the only thing that survived in the area: a glowing beacon in a sea of boarded-up, decrepit buildings.

When I pull into the gravel parking lot, I see one other car. I assume it belongs to whoever is working there. I park next to it and cut the engine. There's a swarm of fireflies hovering around the doorway. I have to swat them away to get inside, ducking as I swing my way through the blinking bugs. Inside I hear old school country playing on the speakers, Johnny Cash or something. I see the cashier is an elderly man, wearing a straw-stitched hat and chewing on a toothpick. His skin is pocked and pale. His eyes look worn and baggy, like he hasn't slept in days. There's a large bandage on his neck dotted with a couple of red dots as if the wounds are recent.

"Hey," I say, walking by and heading straight for the back. The choices of beer are limited to only the most popular American brands. I grab a case of Coors and go to the register.

"That it?" The man asks. He doesn't look at me. His eyes are on a magazine.

Something about him is familiar. I wonder if we've met before. It's certainly likely, since the entire population of the town was small enough to fit onto a football field, probably even smaller now, if I had to guess.

"Yeah." I open my wallet and pause at the debit card, then I move my hand to a twenty I've been hanging onto for a while. It's the last cash I have. I don't even want to think about how much is left in the bank account. I hand him the twenty, noting how the man's hands look even older. It's like there's nothing but skin and bone, streaked with blue veins. It reminds me of my grandfather's, back when he was still alive.

"Have a good one." The man hands me back a few bills and some change.

I stuff them into my pocket and grab the case off the counter. "You too."

I get back to the house in just a few minutes. I can see the upstairs lights are on and can only imagine the shit storm I will be walking into when Natalie sees me holding a case of Coors.

I park in the back this time, near the tree with the tire swing, then mosey my way to the back door. The house is quiet. I pull the back door open and go straight to the fridge, putting the case in after prying one of the cans out. When I look in the living room, I see Natalie sitting on the couch. Her arms are folded across her chest. She looks pissed.

"What the fuck, Daniel?"

"I know. I'm sorry. I just . . ." I hold up the beer can, then snap it open and take a quick swig. "I started to panic."

"You started to panic?" Her voice is sharp.

"Look, I hate this town. I hate this house. I don't want to be here and definitely don't feel like dealing with this." I take another sip. "Then after Deborah took off, I just, I don't know. I needed something to calm my nerves."

Natalie looks toward the muted television, seemingly to look anywhere but at me. I follow her eyes and see that porn is still playing.

"Sorry," I say. "Do you want a beer?"

"Fuck yes."

I grab one out of the fridge for her and sit on the opposite end of the couch, stretching the can out for her. "You know you can change the channel, right?"

She takes the can and cracks it open. "I tried that, genius." She chugs several gulps. "I think your parents have their cable set up to only get porn stations."

"What?"

"There's like ten different ones on and nothing else."

"That's weird."

She snickers. "Not the half of it."

"What else?"

"I took your parents upstairs, hoping they would go to bed."

"You didn't have to do that."

"You left me alone with them. Five minutes after meeting them for the first time." She took another swallow of the beer. "I didn't want to sit here and watch porn with them."

"So what happened?"

"I left it for you." Natalie winked at me. "You should probably get up there soon. It's pretty bad."

"Shit."

She laughs out loud this time. "Exactly."

"Fuck." I set my beer on the coffee table and run up the stairs. I realize as I'm going up the steps that I haven't been upstairs in a decade, maybe longer. The smell of feces and stale, stuffy air hit me with such force I nearly turn around. I pause there, half-way up the stairs, trying to muster up the strength to continue to the top level. I take a few breaths in and out through my mouth, doing everything I can not to smell the air. Then I hold my breath and climb the rest of the stairs. When I get to the top, I choke back some vomit.

"Johnny, you dog!" Dad is naked again, but he's wearing some kind of fake mustache. Mom is naked as well. She's on the floor, on all fours, and taking a shit. I quickly realize the fake mustache Dad is wearing is actually a smear of Mom's shit.

I turn to the bathroom and make it just in time to puke all over the sink. After a few minutes, I get a hold of myself and wash the vomit down the drain. I wipe off my face and take a few deep breaths of rancid air before holding the last one in. Then I go to their bedroom. I can hear Mom mumbling about slugs again. She looks like she's completely out of it, like she doesn't have a clue what's going on.

"Johnny." Dad wipes the shit across his face again, thickening the mustache. "You dog!" He growls as he says the word 'dog'.

I can't do this. I wonder if it's too late to catch up to Deborah. Maybe we can have a few beers and laugh about how fucked up our parents are. I'm sure she'll get a kick out of hearing about this one. It'll give her a chance to get to know Natalie. Maybe they can actually get along and we can all be friends.

As much as I want to leave, I know it's up to me to take care of them. I don't really have a choice.

I go back into their room and immediately grab Dad by the arm, leading him to the bathroom. I walk him into the shower. He doesn't fight me much until the water cuts on. I have to hold him still under the showerhead. The entire time I wash his body he keeps calling me Johnny and dog. I make sure to scrub hard. When I'm nearly done I notice two red marks on his neck, just like the guy from the convenience store. They kind of look like large, scabbed-over mosquito bites. I make a mental note to check on them in a day or two and make sure they are healing properly.

Once Dad is clean, I wrap a towel around him and then grab the toilet paper. I find Mom passed out on her stomach, shit still between her ass cheeks, on her legs, and a pile on the carpet. I start wiping, making trips back and forth to the toilet to flush it.

I dry heave above the sink on the second trip. My eyes are watering.

It takes everything I have to get through it without throwing up on my mother's backside. After I wipe her down with toilet paper I have to wash her with a rag. The entire time, Dad is standing in the bathroom, a goofy grin on his face. When I finally finish, I take him to the bed and lay him down. I struggle to put Mom next to him. She's still passed out and sleeping hard. I cover them both with a blanket, then go over to Dad.

"Goodnight. For the love of god, please go to sleep." I kiss him on the forehead and quickly leave the room, flipping the light switch off and shutting the door as I go.

Downstairs, Natalie is stretched out on the couch. Her eyes are closed. I assume she's asleep so I don't say anything. I go to the kitchen and wash my hands again before finally getting back to the Coors. I don't think I've ever tasted anything as good. I sit at the kitchen table and drink two in less than five minutes.

After getting the third out of the refrigerator, I see something outside. I walk over to the window above the sink. Standing out by the tire swing is a girl. At first I think it's Deborah because of the black, skimpy outfit, but after a closer look I can tell it's not her. This girl is half her age. I doubt older than fifteen. Her hair is blond, almost white. She's spinning the tire, winding up the rope and then letting it unwind.

I check the clock. It's after midnight. Seems kinda late for a kid to be out alone. I try to remember if Mom or Dad ever mentioned her. They used to call and complain about the nurse from time to time, but that was before they went completely mad. I don't recall them ever talking about a kid neighbor. I honestly don't know any of the neighbors and it's miles to the closest house. If she is a neighbor, she's far from home.

FOUR

"WHATCHA DOING OUT HERE?" I come down the steps of the back deck slowly. I'm not sure what kind of reaction I'm going to get from her.

The girl looks up from the tire swing. She half-smiles and meets my eyes. I stop when I reach the ground. Something isn't right. The way she's looking at me. It's like she has the eyes of an older woman, one who can figure everything out about me and my shitty life in one quick glance. I suddenly feel like I'm the child and she's the adult.

"I hope you don't mind if I play with it." She pulls a strand of her blond hair from her face, tucking it behind her ear.

"Play with it? Oh, the uh, the swing? No, that's fine." I try not to sound like I'm terrified of her. "It's just that it's kind of late and you caught me off guard. I didn't even know any kids lived around here."

She giggles, starting to wind the tire around again. "I don't live around here."

"No?"

"Nope."

"Do you need me to call someone for you?"

She shakes her head.

I notice for the first time there aren't any fireflies around her. There are usually hundreds back here near the trees. Shit, there are at least a dozen circling my head right now. But there aren't any around her. It's almost like they are avoiding her.

"Okay." I start to turn around and go back up the steps. I'm not sure what else I can do. I'm certainly not going to call the cops on a girl for playing with the tire swing. I mean, technically this isn't even my house.

"Can I have one of those?"

I look back at her and then to the beer in my hand. I forgot I was holding it. "This?" I lift it up, hoping she will be able to tell it's a beer and not a soda or whatever she is thinking it might be.

"Yeah." She leaves the tire swing and heads toward me.

"It's a beer."

She giggles again and it sends a shiver through me. "I know that. I saw you bring in a big case of them. Maybe I could have one?"

"If I let you have one, will you tell me where you live so I can make sure you get home safe?"

"I suppose."

I know I will regret this. "Come on in."

We go into the kitchen and sit at the table. I hand her one of the cans of Coors. "Take it slow," I tell her and glance back in the living room. Natalie is still asleep.

The girl pops the top and takes a long swig right away. I can tell this isn't her first beer.

"I guess I was drinking by your age, now that I think about it."

"I'm not as young as I look," she says and then finishes the rest of the beer. She crushes the can and pushes it toward the middle of the table next to the other empties. "Mind if I grab another? I was dying of thirst out there."

After everything I've been through today, I honestly don't give a shit anymore. "Sure. Have as many as you want." I chug the rest of mine.

She grabs two and sets one down in front of me. Then she sits, popping hers open. She takes a smaller sip this time and looks at me like she's waiting for something.

"So, uh," I start. "Where are you from?"

"Not far." She takes another sip.

"Did you walk here?" I crack open my new one.

"Yep."

"Should I call someone to come and get you? Are your parents waiting for you to get home?"

"No one is waiting for me."

"No one?"

"I said no one." She takes another sip and then sets her beer down. "I need a smoke."

"I don't have any," I tell her.

"I've got my own. Care if I light up in here?"

I shrug. "Not my house."

She reaches into the top of her dress, pulling out a flattened pack from what appears to be her bra. Then she leans down and slips a blue lighter out from her sock. She taps one out and lights it up, taking a long drag. When she exhales, she sets her pack on the table by the beer can.

"Marlboro Reds?" I ask.

She smiles, that same half-smile that causes a deep dimple in her cheek, and puffs out smoke rings. Her eyes are piercing again. I swear it's like looking at a fifty-year-old woman locked in a teenage body. "You said this isn't your house earlier?"

"My parents. I'm staying here for a bit, I guess. Helping them out."

"Helping with what?"

"They're older. Had my sis and me later in life than most. They've had some issues in the last year. There used to be a live-in nurse, but she took off a couple of days ago. I'm using my vacation time to stay here and care for them until I can figure something out." I stop myself, realizing I just told my life story to a complete stranger.

"What kind of issues are they having?"

"Mental ones. I don't know. I had a lot going on at the time they got diagnosed. My sister was supposed to fill me in, but she just pretty much said they were mad. I guess dementia or something. I don't know. This is the first time I've been here since they got sick." I put my hand over my mouth, cursing internally at how I keep telling her so much.

"Strange they both went mad at the same time, isn't it?" She blows out another few smoke rings.

I notice her nails are painted a dark red, but the tips are chipped like she bites them when she is nervous. "That's what I said to Deborah. She told me she was just repeating what the doctors told her. I think it's really fucking strange, if you ask me."

I finish my beer and get up to grab another. The case is more than half empty. Shit, how many have I had? I glance at the table and see six cans, then another in her hand. I check on Natalie one more time. She's as still as a corpse. Fuck it, let's make a night of it. I grab two more and then go back to the table, sliding one in front of her. "You never told me your name."

She finishes the beer she's holding. "You never asked."

"Well, I'm asking now." I reach out my hand. "I'm Daniel."

"Lilith."

She looks at my hand for a few seconds before reaching out to meet it. When we shake, her skin feels cold. Really cold. I wonder if it's from the beer. I feel a little warm myself. That might be due to the several beers I've had in the last ten minutes.

"Can I have my hand back?"

I realize I'm still shaking her hand, holding it firmly, and finally release it. "Sorry."

"I should go," she says, standing up.

"Are you sure? I mean, are you going to be okay? Should I call a taxi or something?"

She giggles again, then drops her cigarette butt in one of the empty cans. "I think I can manage." She picks up her pack of Reds and puts them back in her bra.

"Let me walk you to the road at least." I stand up and go to get the back door for her.

"I'm fine. Besides, I'm not going that way."

She brushes by me and out the door. She smells like fresh soil. "I'm sure I'll see you around."

I watch her go down the porch steps and across the lawn. She cuts into the field next door, the sacred one I've been terrified to cross since I was a child, and then disappears in the dark. I squint, trying to see which way she goes as she crosses it, but it's too dark to see her.

I turn back toward the kitchen, letting the door close and nearly shit myself when I almost bump into Mom. She's completely nude, standing perfectly still and staring at me. "Mom? What are you doing up?"

"Are you the plumber? I was expecting you an hour ago. I've got some pipes that need to be snaked." She's staring at me, but never quite makes eye contact.

"It's me. Daniel. I'm your son."

"Daniel?"

"Yes."

"Tell the plumber the toilet is backed up again." She turns

and goes across the living room.

I follow her as she goes up the stairs, but when we get to the top, instead of going to her room, she opens the door to the attic. It's a walk-up coming off the hall. She doesn't bother with the light, just starts right up.

"Mom, where are you going?" I switch on the light and go up after her. When I get to the top she's sitting in an old, wooden rocking chair, holding a doll baby and rocking back and forth like she's putting it to sleep.

"Mom?"

"Shh!" She shushes me, nodding to the doll. "Debbie is sleeping."

I'm not sure what to do so I go back down the steps. I figure she'll be okay. Maybe she'll fall asleep in the chair.

I peek in at Dad and he's snoring in bed. Then I go downstairs and pass out on the lounge chair, ready for this day to end.

FIVE

THE NEXT MORNING I WAKE up with a stiff neck and my hip hurts. My mouth is dry and I feel dehydrated from drinking all the beer. I look into the kitchen and see the empty cans still sitting in the middle of the table and can't help but think about Lilith.

I sit up, trying to stretch my neck out. I don't know what I was thinking giving that girl beer. I feel like a dirty creep.

Natalie is standing in the kitchen, looking out the window. I wonder how badly she wants to leave. Before I can stand to go talk to her, I hear the stairs creaking and look over as Dad comes down. He's wearing one of Mom's bathrobes. It's thick and pink and fuzzy.

He goes by me without as much as a glance, then stops one step into the kitchen. "Where's my sunny-side up eggs?"

Natalie doesn't turn around.

I quickly go to the kitchen, stepping between them. "The

nurse quit. It's just me and Natalie here now. So, no more eggs."

He finally acknowledges me. "Why are you here?"

"Good morning to you too, Dad."

"I didn't say nothin' about good morning." He looks me up and down like he despises me. I suppose I feel the same about him.

"The nurse quit," I repeat. "I'm going to be staying here for a while."

"The fuck you are."

"But, you and Mom—"

"Your mother has been dead for ten years."

I hear the stairs creaking again. It's Mom. "She's not dead. She's coming downstairs right now."

"That's not her."

Thankfully Mom has on a nightgown now, though I quickly see it's a bit transparent. She smiles at me as she joins us in the kitchen. Right away she starts pulling pans out from the cabinets. She piles several on top of the stove and then turns on the burners.

Natalie moves away from her and goes to the back door, still avoiding looking at me or either of them. Her eyes are locked on something outside.

I go back to watching Mom, waiting to see if she has any idea what she's doing. She goes to the cabinets and pulls out a bag of sugar and a box of baking soda, then proceeds to dump them out into the pans. I'm about to intervene when she grabs a glass measuring cup and starts filling it with water. Maybe if I had a clue about cooking I would know if she was doing anything right. Instead, I just keep watching.

"Smells like a bar in here," Dad mutters. He's waving his hand in front of his face, trying to fan the air around him. Then he knocks the empty beer cans off the table onto the floor.

"Sorry," I say. "I'll clean that up." I grab them off the floor and put them in the trash can.

"Worthless," he says under his breath.

I have to remind myself they aren't right in the head and that they are my parents. It's my obligation to care for them. Isn't it? I wonder if there is any truth to that.

When I look back at Mom, she's stirring bleach into a pan of sugar water. "Mom." I go to her and take the wooden spoon from her hands. "Let me take over. You can relax."

She seems confused by my suggestion, but doesn't say anything. She walks over to the table and sits across from Dad. I quickly turn off all the burners on the stove and dump the pans into the sink. I check the cabinets and the fridge, but there's so little food I can't think of anything I could make.

"I know I'm going to regret this, but maybe we should go out for breakfast. We can stop at the grocery store afterwards."

Neither one of my parents reply. I turn to them and see they are staring each other down. They look furious.

"Goddamn demons," Dad says. He spits on the table in front of Mom.

She starts growling back at him.

"Why don't we get dressed?" I try pulling Mom's arm to get her to stand. She turns and growls at me. "Fine. I'll bring some clothes down here. Natalie, do you mind helping me?"

"I think you can manage." She's still facing the window in the backdoor.

"Yeah. I got it. I'll be right back." I go upstairs.

Their room still smells like shit. I wonder if I missed some when I was cleaning last night. I move to the closet and try finding something for them to wear. Their clothes are musty and ancient. It takes more effort than I thought, but I find some suitable clothes and take them downstairs.

"What's going on?" I see Dad cowering in the corner of the living room. He's holding a cross that used to hang on the wall.

He has it pushed forward, like it's warding off Mom. She's still growling, but it looks like she's enjoying it now. She's also on her hands and knees again.

"That demon is trying to eat my heart out." Dad puts a hand over his eyes. "Don't make eye contact, that's how they steal your soul."

"Dad, she's not a demon." I lay the clothes on the couch. "Mom, get up and stop growling at him. Come on, I have clothes. We need to get some food before I start growling, too." I help Mom get to her feet and realize I'm going to have to help her get dressed. Fuck, this sucks. I need to hire another nurse, pronto. I lift her nightgown off, doing everything in my power to avoid looking at her sagging, wrinkled body. I realize I forgot to get her a bra and underwear. I guess she's going to have to go commando. Dad, too, unfortunately. When I remove the pink, fluffy bathrobe, he's naked as well. I get them dressed and put Dad's shoes on. I can't find Mom's but I find some slippers that will have to work.

I get them to the car. Natalie walks behind us looking up at the sky. She doesn't help me get them in their seats. Instead, she goes right to the passenger side and sits down. I get Mom and Dad buckled in and finally get to the driver's seat. I put the keys in and the radio turns on with the ignition. It's another ghost hunting podcast. They say they're at some abandoned asylum outside of Pittsburgh. Natalie doesn't make a move to change it, so I leave it on.

After turning around in the yard and starting down the driveway, I look out into the dark field that Lilith crossed through. I don't see any trails or any sign she went that way. I scan the distant trees for a house but I don't see anything. I wonder if she's a ghost.

"I can't believe it's true," Natalie says, finally coming out of her reverie.

"What's true?" I ask.

"There's really no sun here. You weren't joshing me."

"Yeah. It takes some getting used to."

She rolls down the window. "The fireflies are gone."

"They only come out at night."

She leans her head out the window, looking up at the stars. The breeze is whipping her hair around, making the car smell like lavender shampoo. I feel guilty for dragging her into this. I never should have brought her here.

SIX

WAFFLE HOUSE IS THE ONLY restaurant I can find in this hick town. I remember there being more family-owned places when I was growing up, but as I drive around, all I see are boarded up, sign-less buildings. I guess I wasn't the only one to ditch this place come first chance. We pull into the lot and park close to the front door. I can see a few people inside sitting at the tables and one waitress. No one I recognize.

Mom and Dad are eerily calm. It's making me nervous. They haven't been this normal since I got back. We go to a booth by the window and are immediately greeted by an older lady. She looks worn-out and tired. I'm sure I look the same.

"What can I get y'all to drink?"

"Coke," Natalie replies.

"Just water," I say. My mouth still feels dry.

"And you, ma'am."

Mom stares at the table, her hands folded in her lap.

29

"Water for both of them, please," I say.

"Sure thing, hon." She walks off, going behind the counter.

Dad picks up the salt shaker and examines it. "I used to get calls here all the time. Bugs in the salt."

"Dad, stop." I hope no one heard him.

"Look at it. Right there. Contaminated." He brings the glass shaker up to my face, pointing to the middle of the salt. "Spent thirteen years tryin' to rid this place of salt bugs."

"I don't see anything. And you weren't an exterminator, Dad. You worked for the bank, remember?"

"Don't tell me what I did." He pulls the salt back and starts unscrewing the top. "Took me thirteen years and now they're back." He dumps the entire shaker out onto the table. "See 'em. Look at that. It's crawling with the critters."

Natalie looks down into the salt as if she sees what he sees.

"Goddammit, Dad." I start to gather the salt in a tight pile. "There's nothing there. It's just salt."

"That's what they want you to believe. They camouflage themselves. You ain't got the eye for it like me. Took me years to see 'em. I had to learn the secret of their ways."

The waitress returns with one Coke and three tall glasses of water, each with a slice of lemon on the rim. "Oh, don't worry about that," she says, noticing me cleaning the salt. "I'll take care of it."

"Thanks."

Dad leans down to his water, eyeing the glass like he's inspecting it.

The waitress sees him. "Something wrong?"

"No. No. It's fine," I interject before Dad can say anything. "We're ready to order."

She watches him for a few more seconds before grabbing her notepad and pen. "Alright, what'll it be?"

I order some eggs and toast for all three of us, sunny-side up.

Natalie gets an omelet and bacon.

I'm thankful my parents dig right in when the food gets there. Dad avoids his water but seems to have no issue with the food. He eats it all without any more incidents. Mom is being extra quiet, eating slowly, but eating. As I finish up the last few bites of my toast, I see she has a tear running down her face.

"Mom?"

"Call her demon. She prefers that," Dad says.

"Mom? You okay?"

She keeps eating, silently and slowly. I don't see any more tears.

By the time we're all done eating I'm more than ready to go. I'm sure the waitress is ready for us to go as well. I pay with my debit card, wondering if that was all that's left in the bank account.

"Y'all come back real soon."

"Thank you," I say, almost shoving Mom and Dad out the door.

Natalie lingers in the doorway. I look back and meet her eyes. She gives me a little smile and then walks to the car.

It's only a short drive to the grocery store. We pick up a few cheap things, just enough to make sure we don't starve until my next check comes in. I have to keep a constant eye on them. It's like watching a pair of kids. They pick up candy and cookies. Dad stuffs a tube of Pringles down his pants. Mom opens a carton of milk and starts chugging. Somehow I make it through it without killing them. Natalie grabs a few things she needs and pays for her things separately. This time she helps me get Mom and Dad into the car.

The ride home is filled with more ghost hunter podcast. For some reason it seems to calm them. Me too, I suppose. Natalie seems enthralled in it, to the point I wonder if she will listen to anything else ever again. I like the whirling background music they add in. It makes it feel more haunting.

Soon we're home and I walk Mom and Dad up to the back door, holding two bags of groceries. I stop at the top of the porch steps when I see Lilith inside the house. She's sitting at the kitchen table, smoking. I see one of my beers in her hand.

"What are you doing here?" I ask as I enter.

She blows out a long, slow strand of white smoke. "Waiting for you, silly."

"But . . . how did you get inside?"

"There she is!" Mom pushes by me and hurries over to her. She wraps her arms around Lilith's head, hugging her tightly.

"Mom, let her go." I set the groceries on the table and reach to pry her arms off.

"It's okay. I don't mind." Lilith smiles at me. "She gave me a key a while ago. I stop by sometimes and visit."

"Why didn't you say anything about that last night?"

"It never came up, did it?"

I release Mom's arms when she finally lets go. "I guess not."

"Oh, hello." Natalie says as she comes in. "I'm Natalie."

"Sure." Lilith dismisses her.

Dad walks over to Lilith, tapping her on the head like a puppy. "Hello, sweetie. We've missed you." He goes into the living room and turns on the television. It's still porn and the volume is too loud.

"Can I talk to you outside for a moment?" I ask Lilith.

"Sure. Let me finish this off." She shakes the beer can.

"Now."

"Fine." She stands up, blowing smoke in my face. "What's up your ass?"

"Outside."

Natalie looks back and forth between the two of us. I can tell she's confused, but I don't say anything.

Lilith and I go out the back door and down the porch steps. I follow her over to the tire swing. When she gets to it, she turns to me and pushes it at me playfully.

"Stop," I say.

"What's wrong with you today?"

"I don't know, Lilith. If that's even your real name."

She laughs. "What are you talking about?"

"Those are my parents and they aren't well. I don't want anyone taking advantage of them."

"I'm not."

"My mom gave you a key to the house. You're a stranger and she thinks you're her daughter."

"That's just a game we play."

"I mean it. I don't like this. Whatever you are up to, I don't like it. I want it to end."

"Fine. I'll give you the key back."

I hold out my hand. "Good."

"I left it inside." She giggles again. It's the kind of giggle that would normally be cute, but from her it gives me the creeps.

"Tell me where it is."

She shakes her head. "I can get it." Then she takes off across the grass, running inside the house. I can tell she's up to something.

"Wait. Stop." I try and hurry after her but she's too fast. She's inside before I can even get back to the porch. I hurry up the steps and into the back door. When I get inside, the kitchen is empty. I go to the living room and see Mom and Dad on the couch watching television. Natalie is in the lounge chair, flipping through her phone.

"Where did she go?" I ask.

Mom doesn't respond, but Dad looks up toward the ceiling.

"Upstairs?" I go to the staircase and slowly ascend.

SEVEN

BESIDES THE TOO-LOUD PORN playing from downstairs, I don't hear anything. When I get to the top step, I scan the hall. All the bedroom doors are open and so is the walk-up attic.

"Lilith! Stop playing around!" I go to the first bedroom door. It's mostly used for storage now. Boxes and large rolls of fabric lie around the room. I see a dressmaker's mannequin and the old, giant sewing machine my mom used when she was still capable. A tiny twin-sized bed is shoved against the back wall. There are several stacks of magazines and clothing design templates stacked on top of the yellow and orange floral bedspread. I don't see Lilith so I move on to the next room.

"Why are you hiding? What's the point of this?" I move down the hall, wondering if she's a fucking murderer or some-thing. Clearly she's some kind of sociopath, but I'm not sure how far it goes. I need to keep her away from my parents.

When I get to the door to the walk-up attic I peer up the

staircase. It's dark and quiet. I listen hard, hoping she'll give her location away, but there's nothing. Fuck. I've always hated the attic. I take the steps slowly, each one creaking under the pressure of my feet. The hot stink of old, stale air hits me hard. The attic stretches the full length of the house. It's dark but I can see all the way to the other side of the house. Boxes and old furniture are stacked on one side. A brick chimney cuts through the other side. I can see the rocking chair Mom was sitting in, the doll she was holding lying on it. There is an open box of baby dolls just beside that. It's possible she's hiding somewhere up here but I don't see any sign of her.

"Stop playing. Come out, now." The words tremble as they leave my mouth.

I wait, listening. All I can hear is the wind against the shingles. I decide to go back down. Maybe she's hiding in my parents' room. I start to turn around when I hear something. It's not much. A tiny click. I scan the far side of the attic. I can't see anything but random boxes and the chimney. I take a breath and exhale, then start across the floor. The boards are old and shoddy. Several are uneven or breaking free from the nails that held them down. I have to slightly duck to keep from scraping my head on the trusses. The chimney is covered in cobwebs and a thick layer of grime. I stop at the edge, about to peek around it when the door to the attic slams shut.

"Fuck!" I jump and knock my head into the rafter. I go down to one knee and rub my head. I check for blood. I think I just bumped it. There's no open wound. I get back to my feet and move toward the staircase. I glance at the box of doll babies and the rocking chair. The doll from the chair is sitting up now, staring forward. "That's not funny."

I go down the steps and grab the doorknob. For a second I think she's locked me in, but the knob turns and the door opens. The hall is empty.

I run to my parents' room, but I don't see her there, so I go back downstairs. Mom and Dad aren't on the couch anymore. I see them in the kitchen with Lilith. They are sitting at the table, laughing.

Natalie glances up from her phone. She's waiting for an explanation.

"Sorry. Let me take care of this and I'll fill you in."

Her eyes go right back to the phone and I head to the kitchen.

"What the hell are you doing?" I lean against the doorframe, still rubbing my head.

"Relax," she says. "Sit down. I'll make something to eat."

"We just ate. And you need to leave." I move forward, ready to grab her and physically throw her out, but Dad reaches out an arm and stops me.

"Don't talk to your sister that way."

"Dad, that's not Deborah."

"Sit down," he says.

I watch that fucking grin return to Lilith's face. "Dad—"

"I said sit down!" It's the first time he's raised his voice to me in a decade.

Mom and Lilith start giggling.

I sit in the only empty seat and stare hard at her. "I'm going to call the cops. I'm tired of fucking around with you."

"Is that any way to talk to your sister?" Her expression is pure mischief. I can tell she's loving every second of this.

"Stop. Just stop."

"You stop." She stands up. "How about you relax and enjoy a nice dinner with your family? I'll cook." She goes to the bags of groceries and starts digging through them.

My head is thumping, I hold my hand on it and close my eyes.

"I heard the bang," Lilith says. "Did you hit your head?"

"I'm fine."

She puts some chicken on a baking sheet and turns on the oven. "Don't be silly, I'll take a look at it." Then she goes into the freezer and pulls out a tray of ice. She cracks out a handful and wraps them in a paper towel. After she puts the tray back, she comes over to my head. I jerk away at her first touch, still tempted to throw her out. "Hold still."

"I don't need your help."

"Are you sure?" She runs a hand through my hair, locating the bruise. "It seems like you may be in over your head. I'm just trying to help."

"We don't need your help."

Dad points his meaty finger at me. "Stop being an asshat."

Mom starts shaking and I can't tell if it's a reaction to everything or if she's faking it. It looks staged. I suddenly wonder if they are all in on some weird game at my expense.

"Slugs are in the flower bed." Her whole body is trembling now. "Slugs are in the flower bed."

Lilith is standing behind me, holding the ice to my head with one hand and rubbing my shoulders with the other. I'm so occupied with figuring out Mom that I don't notice how long she's been doing it. I imagine she's smiling right now, thinking she's got us all wrapped around her finger. I decide to let her think that. Maybe I can use it to my advantage. Maybe I can figure out what her angle is here, what she's really after.

"That feels good," I say.

"See," she replies. "I'm not all bad. I can help if you give me a chance."

"Well, what did you have in mind?"

She walks over to the oven and starts preparing some sides dishes. "How about we discuss everything over dinner? Mom? Dad? That sound good to you?"

They nod.

"Girlfriend? That sound good to you?"

Natalie doesn't look up from her phone this time. "Sounds

37

wonderful."

Lilith finally looks to me.

"Sure," I say. "Sounds great."

EIGHT

IT'S EARLY AFTERNOON WHEN THE food is ready. I'm not the least bit hungry, but I try a few bites. We eat in silence, well, almost silence. Mom is still mumbling and becoming less and less decipherable. Dad is playing with his food. He's making the asparagus spears fight each other like they are swords being wielded by invisible men. His sound effects are interesting to say the least. Natalie and I are silent besides the sound of us chewing in the quiet kitchen.

Lilith isn't eating. She's watching us, smiling. She hasn't said a word to me about what her plan is to help us out. I've been going over different scenarios in my head, but none of them make much sense. I keep coming back to her being nothing more than a freeloading runaway. My very elderly and very confused parents are the perfect targets. Now she's just got to figure out how to get rid of me and Natalie.

She looks at me. "How's the food?"

"Great." I chew a piece of chicken. "You're a wonderful cook." I hope I'm not laying it on too thick.

"Thanks. I enjoy it."

"Is that what you meant by helping us? Cooking our dinner?"

She giggles. "Among other things."

"Like what?"

"You said the live-in nurse quit. I can take over. You know, do the things she did. Care for Mom and Dad." She rubs Mom's arm.

"You know they aren't your parents. If you drop that bullshit, maybe we can talk about you staying here and helping."

Dad throws a piece of asparagus at me. It bounces off my head and lands on my plate.

"I have no idea what you're talking about. These are my parents. Always have been and always will be. Maybe you're the one who's gone mad."

I try not to snap at her. I have to bite my tongue to keep from cussing her out. That little bitch has some kind of nerve, coming in here and pulling this shit. I smile at her, trying to mimic that cutesy, half-grin crap she's been throwing at me. "You might be on to something. I think I might be going mad." If I squeeze my fork any tighter it's going to become part of my palm.

"Well, good thing I'm here," she says. "I can care for you, too." I feel her foot rubbing up my pants leg. She goes all the way to my thigh before stopping. "Do you need me to take care of you, Daniel?"

My eyes dart to Natalie. Her face is down, still captivated by her phone. Then I look back at Lilith. "Don't flatter yourself." I quickly sit up, letting her leg fall to the floor. I can't keep the game up any longer. I think I might erupt. I take my plate to the sink and drop it in, then head outside. I need some air. I feel like I'm suffocating.

I go over to the tire swing and grab onto the rope, squeezing it hard. I picture her neck in its place.

"Daniel," Lilith says, coming up behind me.

"I need a minute, okay?" I don't look at her. I'm not sure I can control myself if I do.

I can hear her footsteps still approaching. She says, "I have some things to do. I'll be back tomorrow."

"Where are you going? Are you pulling this shit at one of the other neighbors as well?"

"It's not like that. I promise. I care about Mom and Dad. I care about you. Not too keen on that personality-less girlfriend of yours, though. I think you can do better."

I finally turn around and look at her. "You don't even know me. You barely know my parents. We just fucking met yesterday. You're a fucking psychopath!"

She's goddamn giggling again. "I'm sorry, but that is the funniest thing I've ever heard. You calling me a psychopath."

"Why is that funny?" I ball my hands into fists, digging my nails into my palms.

"Mom and Dad love me. I'm their favorite. You're the one they can't stand. If I push I can have them throw you out. I don't really need your permission to be here. I can stay if I want. You, on the other hand, have everything twisted. You think you're in charge. You think you have a handle on things. You are more off the rails than your parents." She pulls out her pack of Reds and the lighter.

"Try some shit like that and I'll have the police department here in five minutes."

"It will be my word against yours." She pulls one of the cigarettes out with her lips, then slides the pack back into her dress. She lights it up and takes a drag. "Plus, Mom and Dad are on my side," she says before exhaling.

"So what do you want? We don't have any money. They've always been broke. I don't have a dime in savings and my real sister is a total fuck up. I think you picked the wrong family to terrorize. You're not getting shit out of us."

She smiles. "It's not about money."

"Well, fuck. What the hell is it about then? You really just need to stay here, that's all?"

"I have my own place. I don't need to stay here. I just want to, you know, to help."

I throw my arms in the air and circle around the tire swing. "Perfect. Great. Welcome aboard."

She takes another puff, watching me dance around in frustration. "I'll be back tomorrow. Try not to get so emotional." Then she starts off toward the field again. I watch as she makes her way across, squinting in the darkness to keep track of her. She goes all the way to the wood line and then disappears into the trees.

Right away I pull out my phone and call Deborah. "Hey, what are you doing tomorrow?"

"Why?" she sighs.

"I need you to come back to the house. There's a situation."

"No."

"What do you mean no?"

"I mean I'm tired of this shit. I'm not going to stay with Mom and Dad while you run off again."

"It's not like that. There's some girl here."

"Girl?"

"Some teenage girl keeps coming to the house and pretending to be you. She says her name is Lilith, but she convinced Mom and Dad that she's their daughter."

"What the fuck are you talking about? I was just there. How did they mix me up with a teenage girl?"

"I don't know. Something's off about her."

"No shit. Why haven't you thrown her out?"

"She left for now, but she said she'll be back tomorrow."

"Okay, call the cops if she comes back."

"Mom and Dad want her here. They gave her a key."

"Fuck."

"Yeah, I know." I kick the tire swing and step out of the way as it swings back at me. "I don't know what her game is, but I think I need help. She's trying to fuck with my head."

"It's a fucking teenage girl. Just scare her. You're forty. You can't handle a teenage girl?"

"Just come."

"You're fucking pathetic. You know that, right? Fucking pathetic."

"So you're coming?"

"I'll see what I can do."

"Say you're coming."

She's silent for a moment. "I'll be there."

"Thanks," I reply, but she's already hung up. I put my phone away and look up to the house. Natalie is standing on the porch by the back door, looking out over the field.

NINE

I WALK BACK TO THE house, slowing when I get close to the porch. "Hey," I call out to Natalie. She looks at me for what feels like the first time all day.

"I can't figure this place out." She moves her eyes to the field. "There's nothing online about it. No other places are dark all the time. It's really fucking weird."

"It takes a while to get used to the constant darkness. It can play with your head."

"The fireflies are starting to come back out." She points to the edge of the treeline where a few yellow lights blink in and out.

"It must be getting late."

"How did you survive this?" She glances back at me. "How did you grow up in a place like this?"

I sit down on the bottom step, watching as more lights appear from the trees. I pat the step beside me, hoping she'll come sit next to me, but she doesn't move from the top step. "It wasn't always this miserable here. When I was little the factory was still operating. I think more than half the town was employed there then. They would even pay the kids for bringing in jars of fireflies.

"I remember everyone bragging about how many they caught or how much they got paid. Deborah and I decided to try it one weekend. We took them two full jars of fireflies, hoping to get enough money to go to the movies, but when we got there, we couldn't go through with it. Something just seemed off about the whole place. It felt wrong. We came back home and released them all."

"Do you know what they did with the fireflies?"

"They used to harvest the bio-luminescence from their bodies or something like that. That's what they told us anyway. It was a hi-tech imaging company called Lucid Light."

"They stole their glow?"

"I don't know how it all worked. Dad said they used the luciferin from the bugs for their imaging compound or something. He used to say the only reason they built the factory here was because of the infestation of fireflies. I guess the lack of a sun causes them to reproduce at a super fast rate."

"Luciferin? Like the name of the town?"

"Yeah. I don't know who came up with that."

"So what happened to the factory?"

"It's still there. Closed down back in the late nineties after all the kids went missing and . . ."

"And what?"

"It's weird."

"Weirder than all this?" She waves her hand around.

"I took off the first chance I got. I was one of the few that never disappeared."

"And what? What were you going to say?"

"It was the adults. They . . . they aged."

Natalie comes down the steps and finally sits next to me. "Aged? Anything more specific than that?"

"My parents aren't as old as they seem."

"I'm not following."

"Have you noticed how old everyone looks here?"

"Now that I think about it, I guess I have."

"My parents have been aging twice as fast as they should be. It happens to everyone here."

Natalie looks up at the stars. "Because of the constant dark?"

"I don't know. No one knows. I don't think it was always happening, just kinda started at the same time as the kids disappearing."

"What happened to all the kids?"

I shrug. "It started back when I was still in high school. Kids kept disappearing. At first there were signs put up and search parties, but after a while, it became this unspoken thing, like the parents just started accepting it."

"And no one did anything about it?"

"Of course they did," I tell her. "They moved. They all started moving. The factory couldn't get enough employees. People started calling Luciferin a cursed town. They all left and the factory shut down. Just a handful of families stayed."

"Like your parents."

I nod. "I guess after Deborah and I moved away they didn't really see a point in leaving."

"And you think that's what caused them to age like that, sticking around here?"

"Yeah. I don't know exactly how it happens, but I know I'm not staying here any longer than I have to."

"Why didn't you tell me all of this before we came?"

"You didn't even believe me about the sun." I laugh.

"That's true."

I reach down for her hand. "Are we okay? I know it's been a

lot to take in. I can tell you aren't happy about being here."

"I was really hoping for a beach vacation. You know, warm, bright sunshine. Lying in the sand. Listening to the waves crash."

"Instead you get total darkness and a psychotic family."

"Well, it's not total darkness." She lifts her hand as a firefly buzzes around it.

"I've had my share of those little fuckers. I'd be happy to never see one ever again."

"Well, they seem to like you."

I swipe one away from my face. "Me? Look at you. They've really taken to you."

She cups the firefly and pulls it in for a closer look. "Speaking of little fuckers, what the hell is up with that girl? At first I thought you had another sister you didn't tell me about, but I guess that's not the case."

"No. I have no idea who she is."

"But she's here and she's a kid. In fact, she's the only kid I've seen here since we got into town." Natalie opens her hand, watching the firefly crawl over her palm.

"I don't know if I would call her a kid. Something is seriously wrong with her. It's kind of freaking me out, honestly."

"What about your parents? What's the plan? What are you going to do?"

"I'll call the agency tomorrow and see if we can get a replacement nurse. Hopefully they'll take a check."

She starts guiding the firefly around her hand, letting it walk in circles over her fingers and then the back of her hand.

I stand up and start toward the house, hesitating at the door when I notice Natalie not moving. "Are you coming in?"

She glances over her shoulder to me for a second, before returning her sight to the firefly. "I think I'll stay out here for a few more minutes."

The thought of her out here alone gives me pause, but I scan the field and backyard and don't see a thing besides the increasing number of bugs. "Okay."

When I turn back to the door, I see Dad smearing something across the window. His fingers are covered in a dark, thick substance and he's spelling out the words 'FUCK YOU' onto the glass. It's written directly in front of my face.

I quickly pull the door open and chase him away. I'm relieved to find that it is not shit Dad smeared this time, but muddied soil from a flower pot. I'm assuming the FUCK YOU was still aimed at me, though.

I grab a paper towel and get it damp from the sink, then start washing the letters off. I can't help thinking about why the hell I'm even here, wasting my time, when they clearly don't want me here. Maybe I should just let that psycho bitch move in and deal with my parents. They sure as hell seem to think it's a good idea. Maybe I should walk away and not give it another thought, leave them on their own. That worked for Deborah.

When I get the window clean, I take the towel to Dad's hands. He's sitting on the couch, putting up a fight, but I eventually get them clean enough. Mom is standing against the wall, nose to the paint like she's in some kind of voluntary time out. I move her to the couch.

I sit between them, watching the muted television. There's some kind of fetish porn on. It's interesting enough to keep them occupied. After a few minutes I pull out my phone and look up the caregiver agency I hired the nurse from. I check the time and see it's after seven, so I assume they are closed. I'll have to give them a call first thing in the morning.

I open my Twatter app and start scrolling through posts, not really paying attention to any of them. It doesn't take long until I'm nodding off to sleep.

TEN

"HOW DOES THAT FEEL?"

I open my eyes. I'm lying on the couch and Lilith is on top of me, naked and grinding. I see my clothes are removed, sitting in a pile on the floor. "What are you doing?" I lift her off, turning my body away from her. I quickly grab my shirt and cover my exposed crotch. I'm embarrassed to find that I'm fully erect and throbbing.

"What's the matter?"

I scan the room, looking for Natalie. I open my mouth and then close it again. Then finally, I say, "Who are you?"

She does that giggle thing. The one I want to shut up with a boot to the teeth. "You know who I am."

"No, I don't." I find my boxers and slip them on, then pull my shirt over my head, squeezing my middle-aged body into it. "You randomly showed up in my parents' yard, remember? We just met. I have no idea who you are. And frankly, I want you to leave.

I want you out of my life and my parent's life forever."

I could see her eyes on my crotch, the fabric of my boxers leaving little to the imagination. "You seemed to be enjoying my company a minute ago."

"I was asleep. I had no idea what was going on." I see her clothes folded on the chair so I get up and toss them at her. "Get dressed. I need you to leave. Where's Natalie? Where are my parents?"

She catches the clothes and stands up, holding them at her side.

I stare at her naked body, taking in her full breasts and tight stomach. When I realize I'm staring, I quickly look to the floor. "Please," I say. "I don't want you here."

She comes over and leans into me, kissing my neck. "Are you sure?"

I step away and walk into the kitchen, going to the back door. I can see out the window that the fireflies aren't out. I check the clock on the wall and see it's just after nine in the morning. "Where is everyone?"

"Mom and Dad aren't here." She follows me into the kitchen. She's still not dressed.

"What are you talking about? Where are they?"

"They went for a walk. I helped them get ready. They were pretty excited."

"They went out by themselves?"

"That bimbo went with them."

"Natalie?"

"I don't remember her name."

"Shit." I run back into the living room and grab my pants, tugging them on as fast as I can. I don't even bother with socks or shoes. Then I run back out through the kitchen to the back door. "Which way did they go?"

Lilith is shaking her head. "You're being ridiculous. They'll be fine."

"Which way?" I slam my hand onto the back door, trying to keep my anger from exploding.

"Out there." She points to the field. "That way."

I pull the door open and take off down the porch steps.

"They've been gone a while, you'll never catch them!" Lilith says as I sprint across the yard.

I run into the field for the first time in my life. I'm not sure why I was so terrified of it before. I remember the stories of the old church that used to sit at the very spot I'm running. I remember my parents warning me to never go near it. There doesn't seem to be anything special about it now that I'm in it. I watch the dirt and dead plants below me as I run, wondering if it was true or just something my parents told me to keep me from playing in the crop. My feet sink in a little with each step. I look up and scan the treeline, then slow down after almost slipping. I realize the dirt is wet enough that I should be seeing footprints. I slow a little more and focus on finding them. The sky is cloudless and the stars are bright. I should be able to see something.

There's nothing at first. It looks like I'm the first person to ever walk through, but I know that can't be right. I've seen Lilith go this way. I must be in the wrong area. I glance back at the house and it seems farther away than it should. I guess I've been running longer than it feels. I try to get my bearings, remembering the way Lilith walked the other night.

I move a little to my right. The terrain is getting lumpier and muddier. It's hard for me to walk. I quickly change paths and it's a lot more of the same.

"Mom! Dad!" There's no sign of them anywhere. "Natalie!"

I pat my pockets, searching for my phone. I must have left it on the couch.

I start running again, hoping nothing terrible has happened

to them. I start to think of the worst-case scenarios. I start to picture them hurt. When I get to the treeline I see an old, metal fence. The wires are rusted and the posts look older than me, but it's all still in tact. I go up to the wire and put my hand on it, testing the stability. It holds, leaving an orange rust line across my palm. I give the post a nudge and it too is still firm. I follow it with my eyes, searching for a broken section. I start walking along it.

"Natalie!"

I test another spot, but the fence is stronger than it looks. It's not tall; I know I can climb over it. I can certainly picture Lilith and Natalie climbing it, but not my parents. There's no way they could get over it. I can't even picture them trying.

I look back across the field, back by the house. I see something moving quickly. A car.

"Finally, Deborah," I say, but right away can tell it's not her car. It takes me a second to register that it's my car. My car is going down the driveway, leaving without me. "Lilith!"

I push through the branches of the few trees between the fence and the field, then immediately start running. I realize she tricked me. She sent me out here so she could steal my car. Who knows what else she took? I wonder if Mom and Dad are with her. I wonder if they are dead up in their room with half of their things missing. It was all an elaborate ploy to steal from them. "That bitch."

I slip and lose my footing, landing hard on my ass. My hands sink into the mud and I stay there for a second, watching my car disappear from view. When I get back up, my entire backside is covered in mud. My bare feet are caked in it. My hands look like I'm wearing mud mittens. I can't believe I let her trick me.

I walk the rest of the way across the field and finally get to the house. I use the outside hose to rinse off my hands and feet. I try to get most of the mud off my pants but just end up soaked and still dirty. I turn off the water and go inside.

"Mom! Dad!" I call for them again, even though I have a feeling they won't answer. Either dead or gone with Lilith. "Natalie! Are you in here?"

The downstairs is empty. I quickly change out of my wet clothes and into a dry pair of jeans and a t-shirt. I toss my wet, muddy clothes on the floor by the couch. I'll have to wash them later. I put on socks and shoes and then search the couch for my phone, tossing the cushions on the floor. Nothing. I look under it, wondering if it got knocked beneath during my encounter with Lilith, but it's not there either.

I go upstairs, expecting the worse. I wonder if she slit their throats while they were sleeping or shot them in the head. I get mixed emotions when I see the bedroom clear of blood and bodies. The bed is made. The floor is clean. The smell of feces is still lingering. I know it will take a deep carpet cleaning to get rid of that. I check the bathroom, wondering if they were left in the bathtub to bleed out. That would certainly keep the mess to a minimum. However, the bathroom is blood-free and vacant. I search the rest of the house and there is no one in the other rooms.

"Shit. She took them."

I go back downstairs, still baffled by whatever game Lilith is playing. I start pacing the living room, picking up speed with each cycle. After a few minutes, I expand my pace to include the kitchen. My mind is racing. I don't understand anything about what she is doing. I can't even begin to comprehend the motive of something like this.

I remember the house phone hanging on the wall in the kitchen. I don't remember the last time I used it. I pick up the receiver and put it to my ear. There's no dial tone. I can't remember when I last paid the bill for them. It was months ago, at least. I hang the phone up and start pacing again. I don't think I could have fucked this up harder if I would have tried.

I stop pacing at the fridge and grab another beer. I sit at the table and start drinking.

After a while I see a car pull up behind the house. It's not my car. It's Deborah in her piece of shit VW. She gets out and comes up to the back door. She looks surprised to see me.

"Where's your car?"

I chuckle. "I know, right?"

"I don't get it." She sits down across from me.

"Get what?" I take another swallow of beer.

"The car?"

"She took my car and left."

"Natalie?"

"No, that fucking girl."

"The teenager?"

"Yeah, she tricked me. I was running around like a fool out there," I point in the direction of the field, "shouting for Mom and Dad. She said they went walking. Then while I was out there, she stole my car."

Deborah throws her head back, laughing. She slaps the table, almost crying with laughter. "Oh, fuck." She continues in a loud, sobbing-like laugh. "That's some funny shit."

"Stop. This is serious. That girl is trouble, you don't understand. I think she took Mom and Dad and maybe Natalie, too. I don't know. None of them are here."

I wait several minutes for her to get a hold of herself. I guess I deserved to be laughed at for how I've handled things so far.

"Are you sure? Maybe they did go for a walk and the girl just took your car to go look for them."

"I don't think so. There weren't any footprints out there. I didn't see any sign of Mom or Dad. I don't know why the fuck Natalie would go with her willingly. It all feels wrong."

"So what's your plan? Wait here for them to come back?"

"My car is gone and my phone is missing. What other choice do I have?" I finish the beer, crush the empty can, and toss it into the over-filled trash bin.

"Let's go find them. I'll tell the little bitch to take a hike." She stands up. "At least one of us has balls."

ELEVEN

WE GO OUT TO DEBORAH'S car and I have to move the trash around the floorboards in order to set my feet down. It smells like old food and possibly body odor. It's the same scent I have always associated with her. My dirty, hipster sister. I roll the window down right away. When she turns on the car some weird electronic thumping music comes on.

"You're not in your twenties anymore, you know," I shout over the music. "You're allowed to act like a grown up."

"Says the guy who got duped by a teenager."

"Whatever. Let's just go."

She turns around and speeds down the gravel driveway. Dust bellows out behind us. I wonder how she hasn't gotten killed in an accident yet. When we get to the main road she drives a bit more under control, though just as fast. It doesn't take long to get into town.

We drive around aimlessly for a while, passing the corner

56

store and a hardware store, then a mostly empty strip mall of boarded-up buildings with a dirty grocery store as the only remaining thing open. After that, there are a few streets of abandoned houses, dark and lifeless, followed by a clothing store with naked mannequins in the grimy windows. I don't see any sign of Lilith or my parents.

I tell Deborah to stop by the Waffle House, I see the same waitress that served us the other day. She's standing outside, leaning against the glass, puffing on a cigarette. She looks like she's given up on life.

"Pull over right there," I tell Deborah, turning down the music as I say it.

"Why?"

"Just do it."

She stops the car, angling across two parking spots. I hang out the window. "Hey." I wave at the waitress.

The waitress rolls her eyes. "I'm off right now, hon. If you have questions you have to go in." She takes another drag and looks at her phone.

"No. I'm looking for someone. Well, more than one."

"Haven't seen 'em."

Deborah pulls me back into the seat and leans across me. "We're looking for an old couple and a teenage girl."

"I came here with my parents and girlfriend the other day," I add.

The waitress exhales audibly. "Look, I only get a fifteen-minute break. I have no idea who the fuck you're looking for and I don't want to spend my break helping you. Sorry."

"Thanks for nothing," Deborah says. She hits the gas and pulls the car away quickly. "What a waste of life."

"I'm sure she was just having a bad day or something."

"Fuck her."

Deborah drives us down the rest of the main strip. It's the

part of town still somehow clinging to life, but even that is pretty sad-looking. I wonder how anyone is surviving working around here. I guess that's how you get people like that waitress. They're all barely hanging on at this point.

We drive to the edge of town, only a few hundred yards from the interstate. The old Lucid Light business building is boarded up, sitting beyond a cracked parking lot. Weeds and small bushes plow through the cracks. Two of the rusted and non-working light posts are lying on their sides. The concrete bases are split and crumbled, with sticks of rebar poking out. Looming behind the building is the dark silhouette of the enormous factory. Deborah pulls into the lot.

"There." She nods her head toward the business building. My car is parked near the boarded-up and graffiti-covered front door. All four passenger and driver-side doors are wide open. As we get closer I can see that no one is inside the car.

Deborah parks right beside it and I immediately jump out. I go to the car and stick my head in, checking for anything that might explain where they are. I see the keys still in the ignition, though the car is turned off. I grab the keys and pocket them while looking for my phone. I don't see it. Then I go around the car, closing all the doors.

"So?" Deborah asks, walking over.

"They aren't here."

"No shit. Where the hell did they go?"

"I don't know." I look around the parking lot and then to the building. I don't see any open doors or windows.

"Do you think they're in there?"

"Could be." I walk closer to the front door with Deborah coming up behind me. One of the pieces of plywood nailed over the door has the words *SATIN WUZ HEAR* spray painted in dripping red. A few poorly drawn pentagrams surround it, along with an upside-down cross.

"Fuck this shitty town."

"We need to get Mom and Dad out of here. That's one of the things I wanted to talk to you about. I don't have the money to put them in a home, and honestly, I can't even afford the nurse anymore. I know you don't have the money either."

"Damn right, I don't. So how the hell are we suppose to get them out of here?"

"Sell their house."

"The house is falling apart, not to mention it's in the buttfuck of nowhere, with the closest town in the process of complete abandonment. Look around you. This town will be nothing but boarded buildings soon. I mean, where is everyone. There's got to be less than a hundred people living here now."

"I know, but it's all we have."

"We won't get shit for the house. It won't be enough."

"It will have to be. They can't stay here."

"Fuck." Deborah pushes on one of the pieces of plywood and it shakes. She gives it a hard pull and is able to slide it open a few feet. "So are we going in or what?"

"I guess we have to."

"We could leave. Drive the car back to their house and call the cops."

"And tell them what exactly?"

"I don't know. Tell them Mom and Dad wandered off."

"Just lie about the girl?"

"I would."

"What if they can't find Mom and Dad?"

"All the better for us."

"We can't—"

"I know. We can't just leave them." She pulls the plywood back even more, revealing a vast, dark space that looks like it goes on forever.

I can't see anything but black. "I don't think they could have gone that way. It doesn't seem possible." I'm about to tell her to forget about it, maybe check the perimeter of the building and see if they're walking around the back, but something moves across the darkness. It's so subtle I think I made it up, like I'm seeing things in the dark that aren't there, but I strain my eyes and focus. I see it again. "Something's in there."

"Yeah, a fuck ton of bugs and rats and shit," Deborah replies.

"I think it's a person."

TWELVE

I DUCK UNDER THE PLYWOOD and into the window. Glass crunches beneath my shoes. At least, I think it's glass. It's so dark I have to stand there a second to get my bearings. I turn around and hold the plywood so Deborah can get inside.

"Did you see where they went?" she asks. "Was it Mom or Dad?"

I let go of the plywood and it falls closed. The inside is absolute dark. "I can't see anything."

"This is dumb. Let's go. We'll never find them in here." Deborah grabs onto my shirt. I guess so she won't lose track of me.

"Wait. Look over there," I say, pointing to a tiny light spot. It looks like a flashlight or little lantern.

"What is it?"

"Only one way to find out." I start forward, holding my hands out in front of me. I can't see the cobwebs and spiderwebs until they brush against me.

"Fuck this," Deborah says. "There's no way they're in here. It's probably some homeless fuck. Let's get out of here."

"We have to check." I keep moving toward the light. I can hear her steps echoing on the concrete behind me.

A dim light turns on, casting my shadow in front of me. I turn and see Deborah has pulled out her phone and is using it as a flashlight. "My battery is low, so this is as bright as it's gonna get," she says.

"Better than nothing." I wait for her to get next to me.

The floor is mostly clear. There are stacks of boxes every few feet or so, all of them unlabeled and taped up. I see a couple stacks of shelving and there are spots where the drop-down ceiling has collapsed. Black wires and yellow, sagging insulation hangs above us, intertwined in cobwebs and covered in dust. I have no idea how long this place has been abandoned and boarded up, but it feels like it has been a decade. We pass a column dripping with water, a dark puddle pooled around the bottom of it. The smell is stale and moldy. I don't see how anyone could think it would be a good idea to spend any amount of time in here.

Deborah moves the cell phone's light to her left in a quick motion, grabbing onto me with her free hand. Her nails dig into my skin. "Shit!" We both jump when we see a huge husk of snakeskin. Judging from the size of it, the snake must be several feet long and very thick.

"Do you think it's still in here?" she asks, relaxing her stabbing fingernails.

"I sure as shit hope not."

Up ahead, the tiny, glowing light starts to flicker.

"Let's keep moving," I whisper as it blinks out.

Deborah digs her fingers into my upper arm again. "I told you this is stupid."

"Someone is in here. We need to make sure it's not them." I

keep moving, shuffling my feet across the concrete floor. I'm almost dragging Deborah at this point.

Without the tiny light I start to lose my direction. I try to focus in on the darkness where I think the light was, but it's harder to pinpoint with each step. Deborah is shaking, which is causing me to shake. The light from her phone is dancing in front of us, only illuminating a few feet and nothing more. I try not to think about giant snakes and focus on moving us toward the spot where I last saw the blinking glow.

Then, as suddenly as it went out, the light blinks back on. Only this time, I can see something near it. A figure—no, two figures. Deborah goes still, stopping us from going forward anymore.

"Come on. It's okay. I think it's them." I pull her forward, looking at the figures, trying to decipher their identity. The shape of their bodies. The size and height. I start to walk faster. I'm dragging Deborah with me, ignoring her stabbing fingernails and reluctant motion. She can't see what I see. She doesn't realize.

The light goes back out again, but we're close enough that I can still see the standing figures. Deborah locks her feet, refusing to move, so I pull free from her grip.

"Mom? Dad?" I stop just before them. It's still so dark I'm not entirely sure it's them. Something looks off about their faces. Maybe it's the lighting, or lack thereof, I suppose. I go to take another step and my foot bumps into something on the ground. It slides a few inches, and I can barely make out the object. I reach down and pick it up. It's the flashlight from my car. The one I keep on the floorboard in the backseat. I switch it on and it blinks to life.

"Mom? Dad?" Deborah sounds uncertain. She sees what I see now, shining her phone light at their faces.

I shine my light up too, examining them. They're standing

perfectly still, like they are in a trance. It's like they're hypnotized or something.

"What happened to them?" Deborah asks, taking tiny steps closer. She's on the brink of tears.

"I don't know. Their faces—they look . . . older."

"They look way older. They look like they're about to die."

I reach out and touch Mom's arm. She's still warm. Still alive. I grab onto her shoulder and give it a little shake, but she doesn't respond. I move the flashlight to Dad's face. His eyes are wide open and staring. It's like his mind is completely gone now. I give him a firm shake on the shoulder too, but he doesn't respond either.

"We've got to get them out of here. We need to call for help." Deborah moves next to Mom and waves her hand in front of her face.

"Where's Natalie?" I turn around and shine the flashlight around us. "She's still in here."

"Maybe's she back near the door, where you saw someone walking?"

I shine the light all around, scanning the rest of the building. It's mostly boxes and stacks of shelving. In one corner there is a pile of broken chairs and a few desks pushed together. Then I see the figure I must have seen earlier. It's far away, closer to the spot we came in, and I can tell it's not Natalie or Lilith.

"What the fuck is that?" Deborah is huddled next to Mom. She's got her arms wrapped around her.

I don't know what to say other than, "I take it back, we need to get out of here." I turn to them. "Right now!"

I grab onto Dad and lead him toward the back of the building. We're able to move much easier with the flashlight guiding the way. I see an old fire exit sign and head toward it. Dad is moving slowly. I have to pull him every step, but at least he's walking on his own. I hear Deborah panting as she leads Mom right behind us. I don't glance back. I don't want to see if that thing is following us. I don't want to know we won't make it out. I don't want to think it's a possibility.

"Come on!" Deborah cries out. She's tugging on Mom with everything she has, barely staying upright.

I finally reach the door, certain it will be boarded up and impassable. I release my grip on Dad and go for the handle. I press hard, putting my whole bodyweight into it. To my surprise the door clicks and opens. I nearly fall to the pavement, landing on one knee. I jump to my feet and yank Dad out as Deborah and Mom reach us. They fall out, tumbling down. Luckily, Mom mostly lands on Deborah and neither one of them seems hurt. I quickly shut the door, making sure it latches, then lean against it while Mom and Deborah stand up.

"What are you waiting for? Let's go," she says.

I grab onto Dad's hand and the four of us make our way around the building. We get Mom and Dad into my car and then Deborah runs for her car. I start up the engine and wait for Deborah to pull away before I follow her. Whatever was in there doesn't seem interested in coming out. I try to steady my breathing and slow my racing heart. I can't stop picturing that thing in my head. I don't know if I'll ever be able to.

THIRTEEN

WHEN WE GET TO THE house, I'm half expecting Lilith to be there waiting for us. Either that or the whole fucking house to be cleaned out. I wonder how much she's stolen already. I park around back, happy to see Deborah is sticking around. She helps Mom out of the car and I get Dad. Neither spoke a word or even moved a muscle the entire ride home. They're both in a walking coma, barely registering the world around them. We guide them into the house and onto the couch. Then Deborah and I sit at the kitchen table. I grab the last two beers and hand her one. I open mine, chugging a third of the can.

"Are we just going to pretend that didn't happen?" Deborah says as she snaps open her can, licking the tip of her thumb afterward.

"I don't think I could if I tried."

"Well, don't just sit there all quiet and closed up. What the fuck happened to Mom and Dad and what the fuck was that thing?"

I exhale louder than I mean to, then take another large gulp of the beer.

"Well?"

"I don't know, okay?" I set my beer down and rub my eyes, still picturing the thing. It was way too skinny, like sickly skinny. Barely any meat on the bone. And its face was fucked. I'm pretty sure it had red eyes. Now that I think about it, the thing's face kind of reminded me of a hairless bat. Kind of pig-nosed with fangs? That can't be right. And the arms . . . god, what the fuck was that? Now we know where the snakeskin came from. I try to shake the image from my head. The dark was playing with my mind, had to be.

"Can we finally acknowledge what's been happening to Mom and Dad?" Deborah points to the living room couch. "It was weird before but now . . . I mean, look at them."

I glance over my shoulder. They look a decade older and that's saying a lot for a couple that already looked like they were in their late seventies. "I've heard about getting so scared your hair turns gray, but this is a bit more extreme than that."

"You think? Fuck." Deborah finally takes a sip of the cheap beer. "They're barely sixty years old and they look like hundred-year-old corpses. I don't think this is from being scared. I think someone did something to them."

"Something or someone?"

"Or both."

I stand up and pace the kitchen. "I have to go back for Natalie."

"She wasn't in there. It was just that thing and Mom and Dad. If she was there we would have seen her."

"Maybe. There were still areas of the building we couldn't see."

"She's probably going on a joyride with the teen girl."

I stop next to Deborah. "Give me your phone."

"No. It's about to die. I need to charge it."

"It'll just take a second. I have to see if she'll answer."

Deborah huffs, then reaches for the phone. "Fine. Just a minute though."

I quickly call Natalie's number. The phone goes right to voicemail. "Natalie. It's me. Call me back as soon as you can. Please, I'm worried about you." Then I end the call and dial my number. It rings for a while before the voicemail picks up. I hang up and hand the phone back to Deborah.

"Nothing?" she asks.

I shake my head. "If that little bitch did something to Natalie ...." I don't know how to end the sentence. I've never thought about killing someone before. I'm not sure I could go through with it.

I sit back down and finish off my beer, thinking of the words I will say to Lilith. Wondering if I should go back to the Lucid Light building, despite the fear of running into that creature again. I can't picture Natalie hanging out with Lilith. I can't picture her going along with abandoning my parents in the building either. I try to think of where they might have gone when a fit of laughter wakes me from my reverie. I make eye contact with Deborah, then we both jump up and go to the living room. Mom and Dad are laughing hysterically. It's a loud, boisterous laughter, the kind associated with mad men. What's even stranger is they're both crying. Their eyes still look lost, staring forward at nothing in particular. Lines of tears are running down their wrinkled and spotted faces. They look even more maniacal, but also sad beyond words.

I look over at the television. It's still off, just their crazed expressions reflecting on the black, dusty screen.

Deborah goes over to Mom and puts a hand on her shoulder. "Mom? Mom?" She starts to pat her, trying to get her attention.

Mom doesn't stop laughing. I can't recollect a time she's ever laughed like this. It doesn't fit her personality. Not since I've been in her life, anyway. I wonder if there was a time before Deborah and I that the two of them had long, uncontrollable laughter fits like this. Deborah keeps patting her shoulder. She keeps calling out for Mom, but getting no response. Then she slaps her. Hard. Right across the face.

"Deborah!" I step closer.

"What the fuck is wrong with her?" She has to yell over their loud laughter.

"You don't have to hit her!"

"I give up." Deborah brushes past me and goes into the kitchen.

Just as she sits back down at the table, Mom and Dad both stop laughing. It happens so suddenly I jump a little. It's like someone flipped a switch, turning the laughter off in an instant.

"Mom?" I wave my hand in front of their staring faces, neither one taking notice of me. "Dad?"

"What's the point?" Deborah says.

I hear her empty beer can crumple. I recognize her tone, she's about to walk out of here and leave it all on me. I've seen it a hundred times. I go back to the kitchen. "The point is that we need to figure this out."

"They're sick. that's it. We can't help them."

"Fine." I sit down at the table.

"Fine?"

"Yeah, I agree. We can't help them. We don't have a fucking clue."

Deborah starts nodding her head. "Exactly."

"But we still need to figure out what to do with them. We don't have the money to put them into a home. And Natalie. I need to find Natalie."

"Natalie's a healthy, vibrant adult. I'm sure she's fine. I know she's your girlfriend or whatever, but this is more important." She points at the living room.

I lay my head into my hands, closing my eyes against my palms.

"Are you sure they can't stay with you until you sell this piece of shit house?" Deborah asks.

"I don't have room. Not right now anyway. Maybe they can stay with you at first—"

"What do you mean you have no room? That big ass house of yours doesn't have room for two more? And you know goddamn well they can't stay with me. That shit won't end well for anyone."

"I lost the house."

"Lost it where?"

"I couldn't pay the mortgage after I lost my job, okay? It took me four months to find a job that paid half of what I was making before. Why do you think the live-in nurse wasn't getting paid?"

"Fuck." Deborah starts laughing now. "That explains a lot."

"Shut the hell up," I reply. "I probably still make more than you."

"That's not saying much."

"Yeah, no shit."

"So, where are you staying now?"

I hesitate to say. "I'm still looking for a decent apartment. They cost more than I remember."

"So? Like a . . ."

"A motel, okay? Does that make you happy?"

"Seriously?"

"Like I said, I'm looking for an apartment. Obviously, I can't take them. The room is barely large enough for the bed."

"Shit. We're fucked then."

"Looks like it." I go to the refrigerator and take the empty case out. "And now we're out of beer."

Deborah stands up. She goes to the window above the sink and looks out over the yard. I watch her, wondering if she can see anything. Then she moves to the back door, checking toward the field.

"Do you see her?" I ask.

"Not a fucking thing. It's always so dark here. I can't see shit. Are you sure this bitch exists? It seems a little weird she only showed up after I left and hasn't come back since I've been here." Deborah moves back to the table, looking down at me inquisitively.

"What?"

"She's real, right? Tell me she's fucking real."

"What are you saying?"

"I saw Natalie. I know she's real, but I never saw this teenage girl you keep mentioning."

"And?"

"It's kind of odd that Natalie is gone. Have you checked through Mom's jewelry cases and shit? Are you sure your new girlfriend hasn't robbed them and ditched them at the abandoned building? That makes a whole lot more sense than a teenage girl mysteriously showing up when only you're here."

"Stop, just stop." I pound my fist onto the table.

"Say it."

"Say what?"

"Say that she's real."

"I already said she's real."

"No. You implied it. You didn't say it."

I pound the table again, rattling the empty beer cans. "She's fucking real, okay? She's a goddamn teenage girl that's fucking with us. She stole my car and my phone and she kidnapped my girlfriend!"

"Fucking with *you*, you mean." Deborah sticks out her hand,

71

palm up like she's waiting for something.

I look at it, then back to her face. "What?"

"Give me some beer money. I'll go get another case. I could sure as hell use another one."

I think about arguing over why I should be the one to pay if she's already talking about drinking some, but I know that would be a pointless conversation. Instead, I reach into my pocket and pull out the last few dollars I have on me. I set them on her open palm. "If there's any change I'll need it back."

Deborah flips through the bills and then turns to the back door. "There won't be," she says as she steps outside.

"We still need to talk about what we're doing with Mom and Dad!" I call out as the door shuts. "And don't be gone long, Natalie might call back!"

FOURTEEN

ONCE THE SOUND OF HER car tires driving over the gravel fades, I sit in near silence. Mom and Dad are quiet. Too quiet. I glance back at them. What the fuck really happened in that abandoned building? Their faces are so wrinkled and drained of life. Their eyes look stagnant and almost colorless. From where I sit it doesn't even look like they are breathing.

"Mom? Dad?" I stand up and go closer to them, leaning in. I think I can see their chests rising and falling, but the motion is so subtle it's hard to tell. I put my hand under Dad's nose, feeling for his breath. It's light, but I do feel it.

I wait around for what feels like too long. I'm starting to get worried about Deborah when I see the fireflies coming out and she still hasn't returned. I feel so powerless, so useless just sitting around the house waiting. I feel like I should be out there looking for Natalie. What kind of a boyfriend doesn't go out looking for his missing girl? I know I can't leave Mom and Dad here alone. I have to wait until Deborah gets back.

Why is she taking so long?

I turn on the television, hoping maybe the sound of sex will spark something in my poor parents. It's another fetish one. Two girls are in a room coated in plastic. One is wearing a collar and leash and the other a solid black mask with a large dildo protruding from the forehead. I sit and watch for a few minutes, hoping it will do something to Mom and Dad, but they don't even seem like they are aware it's on. After a while, I get bored and miss my phone even more. I glance out the window and see what looks like hundreds of fireflies in the yard and no sign of Natalie, Deborah, or Lilith.

I check my Dad's breathing again. God, they really do look like they are dead. It's still early, but I decide to take them upstairs. I don't know if there's any point, but I'd rather get them in their bed than have them sitting on the couch like mindless mannequins.

"Let's go. Come on," I say, pulling Dad up. He stands easy enough and it doesn't take much to get him walking. I watch his face as we go to the staircase. He's staring forward, but there's no life left in his eyes. He really does look like he aged another decade. Whatever happened in that building really fucked him up. I get him into his bed, not bothering changing his clothes. I slip his shoes off and put them on the floor, then head back down for Mom.

"Mom? Are you still in there?" I sit on the edge of the couch, my body twisted toward her. I try to picture her when she was younger—try to remember what she looked like without wrinkles and age spots. I dig through old memories: birthday parties, Christmases, family vacations. Every time I see her, even in the few foggy memories of early childhood, she is still old. Her hair is always silver and her eyes are always worried.

She was never a young mother, that's for sure, but it seems

strange I can't even think of one time she didn't seem old. I scan the room, even though I already know there aren't any pictures of them. There's never been. I see a few of Deborah and me over the years hanging on the walls and one of us together is framed on the end table. Since there are no grandkids, that's really all the pictures in the house. None of Mom and Dad.

I reach over and take her hand. It feels cold to the touch. She slowly curls her fingers over mine. There's no strength in it, they just wrap around, barely touching me. I'm scared to squeeze. I don't know if her bones will crumble under the pressure.

"Let's go upstairs, okay?" I stand up and, with a little gentle guidance, she stands too. We walk up the stairs and I put her in bed next to Dad. I tuck them in and go to the door. I look back at them one last time—the two motionless figures staring up to the ceiling, not moving a muscle—and then I turn out the light. Something feels cryptic about it, like I'm dropping a handful of soil onto their graves or shutting the lid to their caskets. I try not to dwell on the feeling. They're still alive for now, I can't think too hard about anything more than that.

As I head down the stairs I hear the sound of tires crackling over the gravel. I have a moment of fear-induced anxiety before telling myself it must be Deborah. We meet at the back door.

"Took long enough." I hold the door open for her. She's cradling two cases of what I'm assuming is the cheapest beer available.

She rolls her eyes as she passes me and sets the two cases on the table. Her purse falls off her shoulder, keys and change clanging. Then she pulls out a packet of cigarettes and tosses it at me. The empty pack bounces off my chest and falls to the floor. "These yours? Found them on the passenger seat."

"What?" I lean over and pick them up. Marlboro Reds. "Shit. Not mine, but I think I know whose."

"The 'teenage' bitch?" She air quotes teenage for some reason. "The doors were locked, couldn't have been."

"She must be watching you." I toss the pack in the trash.

Deborah rolls her eyes again, then takes one of the cases to the fridge and pushes it inside. I can hear things falling over as she jams it in. I see her eyes move over the living room. "Where's Mom and Dad?"

"Took them upstairs to their bed."

"Do you think that's a good idea?" She closes the fridge and sits down at the table, prying the cardboard case open and pulling out a beer. Instead of getting one out for me, she turns the case toward me so the opening is facing me. "Shouldn't we keep an eye on them?"

"I couldn't take looking at them like that anymore. I figured they'd be safe in their bed," I say, then grab a beer.

"I guess."

We start drinking again. I realize it's the only way we can tolerate each other, and if we're going to figure this out we'll need to do it together.

"So?" She barely gets the word out before throwing back another gulp.

"So?" I repeat.

"You didn't think of anything?"

"No, Deborah. I haven't." I chug half the can.

"I'm serious. They aren't staying with me and I can't stay here either. Fuck this house." She looks around the kitchen like maybe the walls are going to respond.

"I know and I can't either, so that's where we are. Add on no money and no time."

"So we're fucked, or rather Mom and Dad are fucked."

"What do you mean?"

"Think about it. We can always just take off, let them figure it out on their own."

"No, we can't. Besides, I'm not leaving until I figure out what happened to Natalie."

"You saw that thing in the Lucid Light building. Fuck dealing with that. The fact that they ended up there, in that building, with everything that happened before, that's beyond fucked."

I stare at her, exhausted and nearing the end of my patience. "It was never proven that the company did anything wrong. I'll admit there were a lot of strange coincidences."

"Strange coincidences? Almost every goddamn kid in this town disappeared when that place was built. We're lucky it didn't happen to us."

"You think that creature is somehow related to all of that?"

"Fuck yes. I never believed that imaging company bullshit. They probably chopped up the kids and put them in their compounds or whatever, like they were doing with the fireflies. You remember going up there when we were little. They were always up to something sketchy. You felt it too."

I nod. "I never understood. I still don't, but none of this helps us figure out what to do with Mom and Dad or where Natalie is."

She leans back in her seat. "Well, you think of something. I'm not going back near that building and I'm not staying here all night."

I watch her play with the half-empty can, tracing her finger over the brand lettering. I can't even begin to fathom what goes on inside her head. I know she got just as raw a deal as I did growing up. I guess we both could have turned out worse. I don't know why we were spared when all of our friends went missing.

"What are you watching?" she suddenly snorts out.

I look over my shoulder. The television is showing the girl in the collar and leash lying on her back, legs spread. The masked-girl is rocking back and forth between her legs, the dildo on her forehead penetrating. "The cable is fucked up. They only get porn."

Deborah starts laughing, beer spittle flings across the table and onto my arms. "Oh shit," she manages to say. "I forgot I did that."

"What?"

"Yeah, a few weeks ago. I got their account number and called the cable company."

"Why the hell would you do that?"

"I don't know. I was drunk. Thought it would make things livelier around here. I bet the nurse was pretty stunned." She starts laughing again. This time I joined her.

FIFTEEN

DEBORAH CHECKS HER PHONE AND then starts digging through her purse.

"Any word from Natalie?" I ask, watching her maneuver through the junk she's piled in there. A few pieces of paper fall out onto the floor, they look like fliers to shitty band shows.

"Nope." She starts to lift her hand out, shaking loose a charging cord. "Nothing." When she finally gets it free, she goes over to the counter and plugs the cord into the wall outlet. She stays there, leaning against the counter for a moment.

"How long should I wait? I feel like I should be looking for her." I stand up and pace again. "I can't just sit here all night."

"Well, you're not leaving me here."

"I know." I walk back into the living room and turn off the television. I don't feel like seeing any more porn. I don't know if I'll ever want to see it again after all this. I sit in the lounge chair and take another sip of beer. I rack my brain, trying to think of where Natalie might have gone. She did seem unhappy. She never wanted to come here in the first place. I guess it's possible she could have taken off. She might even have sent me a text or called or something. There's no way of knowing since Lilith stole my phone.

Deborah crushes her can and then grabs another from the case. She comes in and sits on the couch.

I'm about to say something along the line of the two of us dealing with this mess with a night of drunkenness, when there's a loud thump upstairs.

"Did you hear that?" she asks.

"Sounded like it came from Mom and Dad's room," I reply. I wait to see if there is any more thumping before getting up from the chair.

"I'll check," she says, setting her beer on the end table.

"Are you sure?" I ask.

"Yeah." She stands up and heads up the stairs. Less than thirty seconds later I hear her shouting for me. "Daniel! Daniel!"

I quickly run up the steps, taking two at a time. When I get to the top I see her setting Dad back on the bed. I hurry into their bedroom. "What happened? What's wrong?"

She struggles to get him into the bed so I move to her, helping to get his upper body back onto the mattress. When he is finally settled, she points to the ceiling. "That's what's the matter."

There's a dark red stain running along the ceiling right where two pieces of sheet rock meet. The crease between them is saturated and sagging. The stain looks like blood, but how it got there and who it belongs to is another question altogether. I watch as the stain starts pooling at one center spot, then begins dripping down onto Mom and Dad's bed.

"Where's it coming from?" Deborah asks.

I put it together quickly and have to steady myself on the

bed. "It's coming from the attic." I immediately fear it may be Natalie—that Lilith has hurt her or worse. I run out of the room, back to the hall, stopping at the open attic door. The light is out and my nerves make me hesitate, but I push past it, forcing myself up the attic stairs. When I reach the top, I turn on the light and scan the room. The dolls stare back, mocking me. I try my best to ignore the ugly things and head toward the area the blood was coming from. Boxes of old things block my line of sight, so I have no choice but to get closer. I realize as I'm stepping over the uneven plywood floor, that this is the same path I took last time I was up here. I'm going straight toward the chimney.

"See anything?"

I jump from the suddenness of Deborah's voice, knocking my head a second time in the last few days on the roof trusses. "Shit." I stop and hold my hand over the bump. There's no cut, but it hurts like hell.

"Sorry," she says.

I turn to her and smile through the pain. "Still looking." I then move my attention back to the chimney. I'm a few feet away now and after another couple of steps I see the blood. It's running down from behind the chimney, slipping into a crack along the plywood floor. I take two more steps and peer around the brick, hoping I don't see my dead girlfriend.

I suck in a quick breath, then continue around. There's a body sitting on the floor, leaning up against the brick. I don't recognize them at first, but I know from the clothes and hair it isn't Natalie. It's a woman, middle-aged. Her dark hair is hanging over her face, shielding it from me. The front of the woman's clothes is covered in bright blood. I quickly realize by the solid blue outfit and logo on the breast that this is the live-in nurse.

I hear Deborah walking over. She stops mid-step when she sees the woman. "Holy fuck!"

"It's the nurse."

"So she didn't run off after all."

"It appears not, but—"

"But what?" Deborah asks. She leans down and moves the woman's hair out of her face. She jumps back when she sees the large wounds on her neck. Two deep holes still leaking blood. The veins around the holes are plump and bright purple. "Fuck. That looks like bite marks." Deborah starts searching around the floor.

I see a weird smiley face drawn in the grime on the side of the chimney. All I can think about is Lilith sitting up here torturing the nurse.

"Look at her fucking neck," Deborah says, starting to sound panicked. "Did that thing from the building follow us back here? You know I can't do snakes."

"I don't know. I'm wondering how the nurse got up here and where she's been all this time." I reach down and touch her arm. "She's still warm. Do you think she was here all along and they just now killed her?"

"You think this just happened while we were downstairs?"

"It looks like it."

"Fuck it. That's my signal to get the hell out of here." Deborah moves around me and weaves her way back to the attic stairs.

"Are we going to leave her here?" I call out.

"You can do whatever you want to do. I'm out."

"Deborah, wait! Stop!" I follow after her. "What about Mom and Dad?"

When I get down the attic steps, I see her dart into their room. I'm surprised to find her standing next to our parents' bed. I stay in the hallway, giving her a minute.

"We don't have to worry about them anymore," Deborah says.

I step into the room. "What do you mean?"

"They're dead."

I hurry across the room and grab Dad's hand. I can tell right away she's right. I walk around the bed and go to put a hand on Mom's forehead. I can already tell before I touch her that she's dead too. We stand there in silence, watching our deceased parents. The only sound is the constant dripping of the nurse's blood falling from the ceiling to their bed.

"I guess that's it then," Deborah says. "And my cue to leave."

"So we're just going to pretend there isn't three people dead in this house?"

"Two of them died from old age, and we don't know what the hell happened to the nurse. Frankly, I don't want to know." Deborah starts to the door. "We can call the cops once we're on the road. They can sort this shit out."

"What about Natalie?"

Deborah shrugs. "We can take one more ride around the town, but after that, I'm on the highway with or without you."

I want to argue with her, to demand she help me do more, but I can tell she's done with everything. If I say anything more I might end up alone here. "Thanks," I simply say.

SIXTEEN

WE DON'T MAKE IT ALL the way down the stairs before realizing we aren't alone. The television is back on and I see Lilith sitting on the couch. She's leaning back, legs crossed, smoking one of her Marlboro Reds. I'm about to start cussing her out, but as I reach the bottom step I notice several figures standing in the kitchen. I stop at the landing. Deborah grabs onto my shoulders, staying behind me. The kitchen is filled with at least a half a dozen of the things from the abandoned building.

"Fuck," Deborah whispers.

In this lighting they are even more grotesque than I had imagined. Their heads are nearly bald: wisps of thin, gray hair stretch from random spots, most reaching down to their shoulders. Large, pointed ears protrude from the sides of their heads. Their noses are pig-like and stout, looking as if they had been slammed up into their faces. The creatures' eyes are red, reflecting in the kitchen light. They stare at us like we're a meal. I'm surprised by their lack of mouths—a patch of skin covers from nose to chin, as if anatomically they should have a mouth, but have mutated into this weird mouth-less version. I thought they'd have fangs, thinking about how they bit the nurse and my parents, but then I see their arms.

"Daniel. Deborah." Lilith smirks, blowing out smoke rings.

I don't even look at Lilith. I can't stop examining the creatures. I can't stop looking at the way large snakes come out of their tattered remains of clothing. Right where their arms should be are snakes; big, wild, writhing snakes sprouting straight from their shoulders.

Snake arms.

Some of the serpents thrash around, agitated and hungry. Others move with wave-like subtlety, rising and falling, searching with a constant flickering tongue.

"Beautiful, aren't they?" Lilith asks as she takes another puff.

I finally look to Lilith. "What are you?"

She uncrosses her legs slowly, sexually, and stands.

I keep my eyes on her face, refusing to give in to her games. "No more bullshit. What's going on? Where's Natalie?"

"And what the fuck are those things?" Deborah asks, barely peering over my shoulder.

Lilith steps toward me. She's smiling with devil eyes and a demon smirk. "Sorry about Mom and Dad, but it was their time."

"You killed them, didn't you?" I stand tall, despite my fear. "You sucked their life away. You aged them until there wasn't any more life left."

Lilith giggles, sounding like a teenage girl again. "Not me, no. They did." She thumbs toward the kitchen where the snake-arm creatures stand, red eyes still ravenously watching us. "Mom and Dad fulfilled their part perfectly. They fed my children for years. And more importantly, they brought you two home to me."

"Us?" I question. "This was all about us?"

"We aren't going to sit around and be fodder for these monsters," Deborah spits out.

Lilith smiled. "Of course not, Deborah." She takes another puff, drawing out the movement. "My children don't feed on their siblings."

I look back to the creatures. I can see the snakes' fangs curling out of their hissing mouths. They look like they want to strike. I move my gaze from the snakes to the faces' of the creatures. I notice something else. It's subtle, but it's there in their mutated features and red eyes. These things are the kids I grew up with, the kids who went missing over the years. "They never left, did they? They never disappeared?"

"They were always here, just outside your house."

"Where's Natalie?" I say, meeting Lilith's eyes. She's standing straight in front of me now. Everything about her appears unnatural. I don't know why I couldn't see it before.

"She's safe."

"Where?"

Deborah leans into the back of my head and whispers just loud enough for me to hear. "Front door."

I try not to react, keeping my eyes locked on Lilith.

"What does it matter? She's so boring. Don't you want to play with me instead?" Her left hand lifts to my face, stroking it, while her right holds the cigarette. She moves it up to her lips and inhales, then quickly blows the smoke in my eyes. "I know you want me."

"Now!" Deborah shouts and darts to the front door.

It's only a few steps behind us and she gets there in an instant. I squint my eyes, looking through the smoke, and turn to follow her. Lilith doesn't attempt to grab me. She steps to the side and points to us as we get the door open and run outside. I hear her speak to the creatures as we descend the front steps.

"Get them," she simply says.

We run out into the front yard, Deborah hesitates at the driveway, remembering her car is parked around the back of the house. I bump into her, pushing her toward the side of the house, making the decision for her.

"Car! Car!" I shout.

We circle the house, swinging between it and the barren field. My eyes can't help but dart over to it as I notice movement. The fireflies are acting weird. I've never seen them travel in any sort of formation or unity, but it looks like they're all flying away from the field at the same time. It reminds me of a flock of birds, suddenly frightened into flight. The fireflies bunch, all moving to the edges of the field as if desperate to get away from it.

Then I see it. The ground is separating. It's not happening everywhere, just certain spots, rumbling piles pushing up. I see something coming up from the soil. At first it's hard to tell in the night darkness, but I stop running and watch. My eyes widen when I figure out what's rising up from the dirt. Caskets. Old wooden caskets. They look like they're floating to the surface, as if they are being drawn up from the deep.

"Daniel!" Deborah screams for me. I turn to her, seeing the panic on her face. "I don't have my keys. I left my purse inside."

I quickly tap the pockets of my jeans and feel my keys tucked at the bottom on the right side. "I've got mine. My car! My car!" I glance back at the field once more and see the caskets are opening. More of the snake-arm creatures are sitting up, lifting their own casket lids with snake-head hands.

"Come on!" Deborah shouts.

I follow her to the backyard and straight to my car. The doors are already unlocked. We hurry inside and I start it up in seconds.

"Go. Go. Go." Deborah is bouncing in the seat.

I put it in drive and quickly u-turn through the yard. Just as I hit the driveway, dozens of the creatures are blocking the way.

"Hold on." I step on the gas and plow through them, knocking several over the hood, and feel a few falling under the tires. I shut my eyes as one smacks into the windshield, cartwheeling over the top of the car. When I open my eyes we have a clear path down the driveway.

"Fuck." Deborah finally settles in the seat. She keeps her eyes on the passenger side mirror, even after I get to the road and turn toward town. "I don't have my phone. I left everything in the kitchen."

"It'll be fine. We'll get you a new one," I tell her. "The only thing that matters is that we got out alive."

She doesn't reply after that. We both sit quietly, listening to the radio. The ghost hunter podcast is playing an episode on a haunted house in New Orleans. I turn it up and try to settle my breathing.

It doesn't take long to get to town and when we do it's completely deserted. Every store is closed and every light is off. I don't slow down until we get through it, coming up to the highway.

"Where are you going?" Deborah asks as I turn away from it. "The highway is that way."

"I can't leave yet." I steer the car across the crackled parking lot of the old Lucid Light factory. "You heard her, Natalie is still alive. I think they're hiding her here."

"We already looked inside the building, she wasn't there."

"Not the office building," I tell her. "The factory."

I pull the car over to a fence that runs the length of the parking lot. We're hidden from the road by the office building, but that also means we can't see if anyone is coming. I spot the gate entrance. It's slightly ajar, opened only a few inches. I consider driving straight through it, figuring the car is already pretty damaged from running into the snake-arm creatures, but I stop just short of it instead. I put the car in park and turn the radio off, leaving the engine idling.

I look over to Deborah. "You don't have to go in. I understand if you want to stay here and wait for me."

"Fuck that," she replies. "There's no way I'm staying out here alone."

I cut the engine and pull the keys from the ignition. "I know she's in there. She's gotta be."

"How can you be so sure? You saw those things coming out of the ground back there. What if they buried her in one of those caskets?"

I rub my eyes with the back of my hands. "No. Lilith brought her here. I can feel it. There's something about this goddamn factory that has always bothered me. I don't know why, but I know she's in there. And she's still alive."

Deborah is quiet for a moment, then says, "Alright. Let's do this."

SEVENTEEN

THE DOOR TO THE FACTORY is unlocked. It looks like someone pried it open with a crowbar a long time ago. The edge near the knob is dented and beaten. Rust lines vein the crumbled areas. I turn on the flashlight I keep in my car, thankful I retrieved it from the office building when we found Mom and Dad. Slowly, I pull the door toward me, holding it all the way open before shining the light inside. Deborah has a hold of my arm again, squeezing so tight my fingers are going numb.

The vast building isn't nearly as dark as the office building was. Sky lights make up a large majority of the ceiling, allowing moonlight to filter through. I can see rows of conveyor belts and big machinery. All of them are covered in thick dust and cobwebs. I take a step inside and shine the flashlight toward the garage door where I remember kids dropping off jars of fireflies when I was a child.

I can almost hear the sounds of the belts and engines. I was always nervous when I would get close to the building. The smell of hot paper and burning ink come back to me. I wonder if Deborah is having the same type of reaction as I am. I wonder if she shared the same childhood anxiety.

There is no immediate sign that Natalie or anyone else has been in the factory for a long time, but I'm not ready to give up. I walk toward a stack of boxes. One on the bottom is busted open, black cartridges spilling out onto the floor. A Lucid Light sticker is attached to each of the cartridges along with some information about the type of ink and compatible printer.

"Just the sight of those things gives me the chills," Deborah says. Her foot kicks one of the cartridges across the floor. It skids through the thick dust.

"Me too. This factory really fucked up our town."

"Let's find your girlfriend and get the hell out of here. I don't want to see this place ever again."

We move through the maze of machinery and production belts, looking for anything that would signal Natalie had been taken here. When we get close to the back of the factory building, I start to lose hope, then I see something odd.

"The fuck is that?" Deborah blurts out before I have a chance to ask her.

A room just off the factory floor is blinking a soft yellow hue. The flashes are rhythmic. It's a steady pattern of on and off, reminding me of the fireflies. A door stands between us and the room, but a small glass panel window cut out on the top half of the door allows us to see the blinking yellow light. I lead the way over to the closed door. When we are close, I peer through the panel window and see a chair facing the wall, tubes and wires sprouting out of it. Someone is sitting in the chair. My someone. *My Natalie.*

I reach for the handle and turn it, throwing the door open. I rush inside before Deborah can stop me.

"Wait!" she calls out, but I'm already running to the chair.

I can see the wires going into a metal helmet strapped to her head. The tubes run into her arms, puncturing her skin and filling her blood with whatever substance is streaming through it. I stop just before her, gasping at the state she is in. Her skin is glowing all around the tubes. Nearly her entire left arm is changed. Her fingers are melding together, turning her hands into . . . into . . . I squint at the realization that her hands are becoming snake heads. I can see the tiny pricks of teeth forming on the inside of her palms and fingers. I look to her face. Her eyes are already reddening—staring out lifelessly. Her nose is crumpled. Her lips have lost all color and appear to be melting together like dripping wax.

"Natalie." I fall down to my knees beside her, placing a hand on her leg. She doesn't acknowledge me, like she's completely unaware of my presence.

Deborah takes a step into the room. "Daniel. Daniel."

I turn to her, doing everything I can to keep from crying.

"We have to go," she says.

I nod, finding the strength to get back up to my feet. "Help me get her."

Deborah glances back into the factory, then rushes over, embracing me in a hug. I think this may be the first time we've hugged as adults. I try to remember another time but can't think of one. I know it's more than her comforting me about Natalie. I know this is about everything. About all the shitty things we've both been through during our lives.

When she releases me, I turn to Natalie. I start with the helmet straps, unfastening them from below her chin. I'm not sure if the wires are live or exactly how much electrical currents are running through them, so I'm careful not to touch anything but the leather straps holding it on to her. Deborah reaches down to the tubes running into her morphing arms. She grabs a firm hold of one that connects to Natalie's nearly scale-covered forearm and yanks it hard. The tube plucks out, pouring a yellow, glowing substance with the consistency of a soupy sauce. The puncture wound oozes a mixture of blood and the bright, luminescent liquid. She tosses the tube to the side, letting the stuff spill to the floor, then moves to the next one.

"Natalie?" I ask, removing the helmet from her head.

Her eyes look like they are covered in a red-tinted film. Her dilated pupils start darting around as if she is coming out of a trance. Then a soft moan escapes, followed by several murmuring, panicked grunts. I realize her mouth has started to seal closed.

I grab a hold of her face, trying to get her to focus on me. "Natalie. Look at me. Natalie."

"Fuck. Hold her down!" Deborah shouts when Natalie starts flailing her arms and body.

I move my hands down to her upper arms, trying to steady them while Deborah pulls the last two tubes out. "Natalie. It's me. It's Daniel." I try meeting her eyes, but they are all over the place. "We're getting you out of here."

Once she is completely free from all the tubes and wires, I put my arms under her and lift her from the chair.

Deborah picks up the flashlight from the floor, leading us back into the main part of the factory. I struggle to move quickly, doing everything I can to keep a hold of Natalie. Her arms and legs are still kicking and shaking. She's grunting and moaning between muffled cries.

We weave through the conveyor belts and machinery, nearly back to the front door, when Natalie strikes me in the side of the head. It jolts me hard enough that I drop her. I lift a hand to the spot where she hit me and feel wetness. When I look down at her I see two little, yellow eyes on the top of her hand. From the forearm down it looks like her right arm is all snake. I realize her snake hand must have bitten me. Natalie looks as startled as I do. Her eyes widen at the sight of the fully formed snake hand. Its tongue is flickering in and out rapidly.

"What's wrong?" Deborah notices us falling behind and comes back.

"She bit me," I say, pointing to the snake.

"Look at her. We got here too late!"

Natalie glances between us, really acknowledging us for the first time. Her eyes are pleading with us for help.

"No. She's still in there. She isn't fully changed yet."

"She bit you." Her eyes are on the blood. And then to my hair with a confused expression. "Your hair is graying. It's literally graying right in front of me."

"I don't think she meant to bite me. I don't think she can control the snake yet."

Natalie started nodding, mumbling behind her sealed lips.

"Can you stand? Can you walk?" I ask, wanting to reach down and help her but hesitating.

She keeps nodding, then starts to stand.

"Alright. Let's keep going." Deborah starts back toward the door.

I stay as close as I can to Natalie without getting in striking distance, hoping she understands what's going on. "Come on. This way. I'm taking you home."

Deborah steps through the door first, disappearing from my view. I move back and let Natalie go next, then quickly follow her. I'm only two steps out the door when I see Deborah stopped. She drops the flashlight to the cracked pavement. The light is still shining, illuminating Lilith and a line of more than a dozen of the snake-arm creatures. Behind us, the door to the factory slams shut. I spin and see several other creatures now circling around.

Natalie lets out a muffled scream and falls to the pavement as if she's lost all hope.

Lilith starts clapping. She's doing her half-grin smirk again and looks nothing like a teenage girl anymore. All I see now is the demon she really is. The demon that has been toying with me since I got here.

EIGHTEEN

"WE JUST WANT TO LEAVE. You'll never see us again."

Lilith stops clapping and steps forward. She doesn't look at Deborah or Natalie. Her eyes are only on me.

I stare right back at her. "You got my parents. You can have the house. Take everything, just let us leave."

"It was always about you. You know that. We could have had a great time. I was willing to spare you, for a while anyway. Take you as my lover." She reaches to my face again, laying her hand on my cheek. She moves in like she is about to kiss me.

I pull my head back, turning away from her. "I don't want anything to do with you."

"Very well. You two are the last remaining seedlings. Soon I will have all of my children with me." She nods to the snake-arm creatures and they close in, trying to grab us with their snake mouths.

Deborah fights, trying to break through them until deep bites secure her arms. She screams out in pain and frustration before finally submitting. Natalie doesn't fight them. I can tell she's given up, knowing there's probably no way to reverse whatever has happened to her body.

When two of the things reach for me I brace for the bite. Their large snake-head hands clasp down on my forearms. I wait for the pain of the puncturing teeth, but it doesn't come. The snakes are clamping down tight, but no teeth penetrate my skin. They pull us back to the factory.

Just before we reach the door, a strange humming sound begins. I look up into the sky, trying to make out a plane or helicopter. I don't see anything, except . . .

"What is that?" Lilith asks, she sees it too.

A large black cloud is moving across the parking lot. It's heading toward us. As if on cue, thousands of tiny yellow lights start to blink on and off, creating a wave-like motion of light throughout the dark, approaching cloud. A swarm of fireflies.

"Get them inside, quickly!" Lilith seems startled.

The snake-armed creatures push us through the door and into the factory. The sound of the humming doesn't dampen. In fact, it increases as if they are nearly upon us. Lilith shuts the door and locks it. Her eyes dart around the large room. "Take them to the back. Let's get this over with."

Natalie finally starts to struggle, realizing they are taking her back to complete the transformation process. Deborah sees her fighting and starts to do the same, kicking her legs and trying to pull her arms free from the snake mouths.

The hum of the fireflies gets so loud it's hard to believe the sound is coming from insects. Then a tiny ping smacks the door. Several more follow. Soon the tiny pings become a barrage of thumping and pounding.

"Go," Lilith says, directing them away from the door.

We're halfway across the factory when the moonlight streaming in from the skylights goes out. I look up and see the cloud of bugs covering the windows. It doesn't take long for the glass to start to shake and crackle.

"Hurry! To the room."

The snake-armed creatures pull us faster, shuffling around the conveyor belts and machinery. Right when we get to the doorway of the room, the skylights burst, shattering glass down onto the floor. I look up and see the fireflies pouring in through the windows like dark liquid. They move in unison, like one solid being. The swarm turns toward us, but can't reach us before we are shut inside the back room.

"Strap them to the chairs. Get the luciferin in them. We don't have much time."

As soon as we are locked down in the chairs, the fireflies hit the door. It sounds like rushing water. I can sense the unease in Lilith. This isn't something she's prepared for. Maybe we can use it to our advantage. If we can just hang on long enough for the bugs to get in, maybe we can escape. I start thrashing, moving my arms and legs and swinging my hips as best I can. The straps holding my ankles and wrists are tight, though I can move the rest of my body easily enough.

Deborah sees me and does the same. One of the snake-armed creatures is trying to inject her with a needle, but she won't hold still. Two other creatures move in to assist.

"Keep fighting!" I shout.

Natalie looks at me. As grotesque and fucked up as she's become, I can still see the girl I used to know. I can still see the human in her eyes. "Fight!" I cry out.

She listens and starts thrashing around too, refusing to give up.

The door is straining on the hinges and frame. It won't be long now.

"Finish it!" Lilith shouts. She rushes over to Natalie and

snatches the needle from one of the creatures. She sits on Natalie's forearm and leans her body onto her, pining Natalie's arm down. Then she inserts the needle and slides the tube of luciferin into it. The yellow glowing liquid starts to seep inside Natalie's blood. After a few seconds, all the fight is gone and Lilith gets off her.

Deborah and I are slowing down, exhausted from the struggle. There are too many of the creatures. Right as I am about to give up, the door to the room flies open, rattling across the floor. A black mass, dotted with rapidly blinking yellow lights, fills the room in an instant. The tiny bugs are everywhere, filling every inch of the room. I quickly shut my eyes and hold my breath, feeling them cover me. I hold in a scream, as the sound of their humming is so loud I can barely take it.

I feel my arms being pulled. It's subtle at first, then a strong jerk nearly rips my arm from the socket. I try to stay in the chair, but the force of the pull is so strong I can't hold myself back. I realize the straps holding my wrists and ankles must have been unfastened during the chaos because I can move them now. I risk opening my eyes, just a slit in order to see what is happening, but all I see is the black mass of fireflies so I quickly shut them back.

They yank me up onto my feet and pull me forward. I scamper blindly. I can tell it isn't the snake-armed creatures holding me. There are no teeth and no feeling of getting bitten. I wonder if the bugs themselves have somehow formed together into a makeshift hand and are grabbing me. I wish I could call out for Deborah and Natalie. I want to see if they are released too, but I don't dare open my mouth with all the fireflies covering me.

I stop fighting against the tugging and let it pull me. It feels like I'm walking for a while before the weight of the bugs on my face and head start to disperse. I try opening my eyes again and see the parking lot outside the factory. I see my car just feet away. Fireflies are still all over my shirt and pants. They slowly fly off, scattering in different directions, no longer staying in a tight formation.

A loud strain of metal and wood come from the decrepit factory. A few snaps and pops echo from inside before I hear pieces of the ceiling falling in. I turn back to look and see a large crack run down the front of the building as it begins to shake and rumble. I take several steps back as the walls collapse inward. It sounds like an explosion. Dust and smoke bellow out into the air and all around me. Bricks and metal beams crumble into nothing more than a rubble pile. When the smoke and dust settle, I scan the pile for a sign of life, hoping I'm not the only one to survive.

"Daniel," I hear Deborah say from behind me. I spin toward the sound of her voice and embrace her in a tight hug.

"Are you okay?" I ask.

"Yeah. I think so."

I see Natalie, or at least what is left of her, standing off to the side. The fireflies are leaving her body, flying off her nearly fully formed snake arms. Her right arm looks completely transformed. Its head is up, tongue flicking in and out. The left arm is scaly with one eye. Its mouth still kind of looks like a hand, though. I can see the bones of her fingers through the scales. Her face is bat-like and bald, with pointed ears and red eyes. I can barely make out some of her features, but mostly, she looks like the rest of the creatures. She's staring at me, and it's tearing me up inside.

"I'm so sorry," I mumble.

Deborah releases me and turns to Natalie. "We have to get out of here."

"I know, but I can't leave her."

Deborah nods and reaches out to Natalie. I do the same. She takes tiny steps forward, unsure of herself, but when she's close enough I slip my arm under her snake and Deborah takes her mutated left hand. We walk together to the car.

The fireflies are still lingering around as the dust from the fallen factory clears. It's as if they are protecting us. I look up at them, watching them blink against the dark sky. I nod, hoping they understand my appreciation. I try not to think too hard about how or why they saved us. I'm just thankful they did.

Deborah helps me load Natalie in the back seat, and then we get into the car. I start it up and peel out of the parking lot. It doesn't take long to get back to the highway. We stay silent until I glance in the rearview mirror and see Natalie squirming in the back seat. I make eye contact with her as she mumbles something incoherent.

"What does she want?" Deborah asks.

Then I see her motion to the front seat. I realize what she wants and turn on the radio.

"Ghost hunters," I say and sit back, listening to three hillbillies talk about a haunted coal mine in West Virginia.

NINETEEN

WE DRIVE STRAIGHT TO OUR motel room. Deborah waits in the car, her finger rapping the dashboard. Natalie is hesitant, but eventually joins me inside. I gather all of our suitcases, filling them with clothes and shoes. Natalie attempts to get everything from the bathroom. I can hear her muffled curses as she drops as much as she picks up. I stop packing the suitcases and watch her, wondering if I should help or if that would just exasperate the situation. I can't imagine how difficult all this must be for her.

She stops suddenly and I realize she's staring at herself in the mirror. Her partially transformed hand brushes along her bat-like face. The tip of her fingers/snout of the snake linger on the stretched patch of skin that used to be her mouth.

"Muhhrrr!" She drops the toothbrushes onto the dirty tile floor.

I move from the bed and the suitcases and step to the bathroom, leaning down to grab the brushes. Her snake-head hand bumps me and I quickly withdraw my hand. The fear of the creatures of Luciferin is still haunting me. I try to play it off like I'm not terrified of her, that she isn't as hideous as they were, but my face gives me away.

Natalie stands up and throws all of her makeup onto the floor. A weird primal-like noise reverberates from her chest, unable to be vocalized. She stomps her feet and slams her hands onto the sink. Then she grabs my can of shaving cream and slams it into the mirror. The glass shatters, scattering the room with tiny shards. I shield my face, feeling pieces fall over me, then back out of the bathroom.

Natalie falls to her knees and starts crying hysterically. Her red eyes fill with tears. Her pig-like nostrils flare out with each whimper. She reaches for a large shard of the mirror, biting onto it with her snake hand.

"Natalie, no!" I move for her, grabbing the neck of her snake arm as she is about to thrust the shard into her neck. We battle for a few seconds, until she gives up and lets me pull her arm back. Once it's clear I won't let her stab herself, she drops the glass onto the floor and wraps her arms around me.

She's mumbling something. I assume she is apologizing.

"It's okay. You're going to be okay," I say and immediately feel guilty about lying to her. She obviously won't be okay. She'll never be okay.

Over the next several minutes we pack up the rest of our things and load them into my car. Deborah seems to be relieved when we get back and start moving again. I glance at Natalie from the rearview mirror, studying her as I drive. I know I will have to keep an eye on her from now on.

Luckily, Deborah has a spare key she keeps under the front door mat. Her apartment is tiny. Natalie and I have to sleep in the living room. I take the couch and she sleeps on a blow-up mattress on the floor. The first night is the most awkward. I watch her until she falls asleep. Her snake arm becomes more awake at night, slithering as far as it can reach, investigating everything around her. When it notices me, I stay perfectly still, hoping it loses interest.

Eventually I pass out, sleeping for several hours.

"Daniel!" I hear Deborah scream and sit up in a bolt.

"What's wrong?" I see her panicked face and then check on Natalie. She's still lying on the floor, just now coming to.

Deborah lifts a shaking finger and points to my face.

"What?" I stand up off the couch and go to the mirror hanging on the wall. I rub my eyes, hoping they're still blurry, because what I see is startling: my hair is completely white, my skin looks wrinkled and worn, sagging below my eyes. I appear to have aged twenty years. Then, I suddenly feel a stinging sensation on my neck and turn my head to get a better look. Two reddened and puffy marks dot the side of my neck.

Bite marks.

I spin around and look at Natalie. Her dark, red eyes stare back, nothing human in them. Her snake arm lifts up, almost smirking at me.

"We have to kill her," Deborah says, finally calming down. "We have to. She'll kill us if we don't."

I swallow hard and nod to my sister. "I know."

Natalie doesn't respond. I wonder if she can even understand us anymore. If she does, she isn't letting on.

I go back to the couch, keeping a safe enough distance that her snake can't strike me, then pull the blanket off. I circle around Natalie, both her and the snake watching my every move. "When I say so, jump on her."

Deborah takes a step closer.

I hold the blanket up, stretching my arms wide. "Ready?"

Deborah nods. "Do it."

I hesitate a second, and then throw the blanket over Natalie, smothering her in it. "Go!"

Deborah takes two steps and then plows into us, wrapping her arms around Natalie's body. She squeezes tight when Natalie and the snake struggle. The three of us fall to the floor. Natalie is kicking and flailing, but she isn't strong enough to get free. When she finally stops fighting, Deborah reaches to the side table, barely able to get the drawer open. She reaches inside and pulls out a roll of duct tape.

"You got her?" she asks.

"Just move quick."

Deborah scratches at the tape until she gets the end free, then pulls a large amount free from the roll. She starts at Natalie's shoulders, wrapping the tape around her. I'm able to move Natalie from side to side to allow the tape to get around her fairly easily. It takes only a few minutes to get her secure.

"Now what?" I ask, standing up and breathing harder than I have in a while. It's going to take some time to get used to suddenly being in a sixty-year-old body.

"I don't fucking know. We dispose of her." Deborah shrugs her shoulders.

"Dispose of her?" I repeat. "What does that even mean?"

"We dump her somewhere."

"I don't know if I can just dump her."

"You saw her face. That thing isn't your girlfriend anymore. She's changed into one of the creatures." She points to the body bundled on the floor. "If we don't kill her, she'll suck the life out of us or someone else."

"I know. I know. But I just can't dump her somewhere."

"Well, what the fuck do you want to do with her?"

I look down at Natalie's red eyes. As much as I want to see a sign that she's still the girl I knew, I don't see anything but an emotionless creature. "Help me load her in the car and I'll do the rest."

Deborah eyes me carefully. "And what exactly are you going to do?"

"I know this is going to sound crazy, but . . ."

We load Natalie into the back seat of my car, leaving her bound. I move the blanket down from her face so she can see. She flinches in the bright morning sunlight as if her eyes are meant for darkness and the sun is damaging them. Her skin doesn't seem bothered by it, just her eyes, so I dig through her bag and find her sunglasses. They don't fit like they used to but I get them to stay on her head. I pull out her bikini and sunscreen and place them on the floor board, then shut the back door.

Deborah gives me a big hug. It still feels weird when we touch, but a nice weird. "Are you sure about this?" she asks.

"Yeah. I think so."

"Have fun, I guess." She smiles awkwardly. "And don't be a stranger."

"I'll call you when we get there," I say and then get into the car.

"Drive safe."

I wave as I pull away, leaving the windows down so the breeze can fill the car.

Natalie mumbles something from the backseat. I think she's excited.

"We're finally getting our beach vacation," I tell her. "It's gonna be a blast!"

Bio

J. Peter W. writes bizarro, horror, and dark fantasy books. He currently resides in Richmond, VA writing with night eyes and night fingers.

Other than writing, he loves graphic design, gardening, playing music, and spending time with his family.

When he retires, he plans on building an elaborate garden labyrinth in his backyard filled with strange statues and weird animatronic figurines.

Other Grindhouse Press Titles